"Right now I'm an open book," Brad said, leaning back in his chair, his vivid eyes sparkling in the light from the setting sun.

He was, too—enough so to start a slow curl in the very pit of her stomach. Lauren hadn't been without male friends over the years, but none of them had made her feel the way he was making her feel right now. The way he'd made her feel from the moment he opened the door to her this afternoon, if she were honest about it. The antagonism had been more in the way of defense than anything. If it weren't for Kerry...

If it weren't for Kerry she wouldn't be here to start with, came the reminder. *She* had to be her only concern.

"I think it's time I turned in," Lauren said.

"Running away?" Brad taunted as she pushed back her chair to get to her feet.

"In need of a good night's sleep," she countered. "It's been a long day."

His shrug was philosophical. "There's always tomorrow...."

KAY THORPE was born in Sheffield, England in 1935. She tried out a variety of jobs after leaving school. Writing began as a hobby, becoming a way of life only after she had her first completed novel accepted for publication in 1968. Since then she's written over fifty, and lives now with her husband, son, German shepherd dog and lucky black cat on the outskirts of Chesterfield in Derbyshire. Her interests include reading, hiking and travel.

Kay Thorpe

MOTHER AND MISTRESS

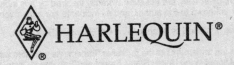

HARLEQUIN®

TORONTO • NEW YORK • LONDON
AMSTERDAM • PARIS • SYDNEY • HAMBURG
STOCKHOLM • ATHENS • TOKYO • MILAN • MADRID
PRAGUE • WARSAW • BUDAPEST • AUCKLAND

ISBN 0-373-18824-2

MOTHER AND MISTRESS

First North American Publication 2004.

This edition published by arrangement with Harlequin Books S.A.

® and TM are trademarks of the publisher. Trademarks indicated with ® are registered in the United States Patent and Trademark Office, the Canadian Trade Marks Office and in other countries.

Visit us at www.eHarlequin.com

Printed in U.S.A.

CHAPTER ONE

THE house she'd come so far to find lay hidden from the road behind a stand of chestnut trees. Tall stone pillars supported wrought-iron gates unexpectedly left open. Lauren drove on through without pause for reflection, following the long, curving driveway through the trees to emerge on a wide forecourt set around a tumbling fountain.

Long and low, its old stone walls bedecked with ivy, its mullioned windows glinting in the sun, Ravella was one of the loveliest places she had ever seen. She sat there for several moments just taking in the picture it made against the backdrop of rolling green Cotswold hills and clear blue skies. Worth a couple of million at least on the open market, she imagined, which gave all the indication needed of the owner's standing in the world.

She fought down the urge to cut and run, and got out of the car. The chances of success might be remote, but any chance at all was surely worth taking. How else was she to gain access?

The big brass bell pull created a sound scheduled to carry to the furthest reaches of the house. Anticipating a lengthy wait, she was startled by the prompt opening of the solid oak door, gazing in sudden confusion at the man standing there. Tall, dark and ruggedly attractive, he was instantly recognisable from the newspaper clipping she'd been sent. The last person she would have anticipated answering the bell was the master of the house himself. It was too soon. Too precipitate!

'Hello?' he said agreeably. 'Can I help you?'

Lauren found her voice again with an effort. 'I hear you're in need of a temporary carer for your daughter, Mr Laxton?'

Vivid blue eyes regarded her quizzically for a lengthy moment, taking in every detail of her striking features beneath the tumbled wheat-gold hair in a manner that raised faint flags of colour in her cheeks.

'Where did you hear that?' he asked at length.

'I'm staying at the village pub. The landlord mentioned it. I realise it's a highly unorthodox way of applying for a job,' she hastened to add.

'It certainly is,' Brad Laxton agreed drily. 'You're not local, for certain.'

'I *am* English,' she said. 'I've lived a number of years in Canada, hence the accent I hadn't even realised I'd picked up. I still hold a British passport.'

She shifted uncomfortably from foot to foot, on the verge of giving up on the whole idea. It had been a mad idea to start with. Who in their right mind would even consider taking on a total stranger who appeared on the doorstep—especially where a child was concerned?

'You'd better come in,' he said, freezing the apology already forming on her lips. 'Obviously I'll need to know a lot more about you before coming to any decision.'

Lauren found her feet moving her forward of their own accord, her lips forming a smile she could only hope didn't look as strained as it felt. Confidence had to be the keynote if she was to succeed in her quest. Brad Laxton might be desperate, but he wasn't the type to throw caution entirely to the winds.

The house was as lovely inside as out, the reception hall lined with linenfold panelling, the furnishings glowing with lovingly applied beeswax. Rising from the centre to split into two wings, a grand staircase gave access to open galleries.

Brad Laxton opened a door on the right and ushered her through into what appeared to be a combination of a study and a library, with book-lined walls and a mahogany desk under the window. A side desk holding a variety of computerware struck the only incongruous note.

He indicated the sofas set on either side of a wide stone hearth, the latter at present filled with flowers in lieu of the log fire that would probably blaze there in winter.

'Have a seat, and tell me about yourself.'

Lauren did so, forcing herself to sit back against the cushions in apparent relaxation as he took a seat opposite. The urge that had brought her this far was fast receding, leaving her in limbo when it came to finding the necessary words. Like blue gimlets, those eyes of his unnerved her even further. She had a feeling he could see right through her.

'So?' he invited. 'Supposing we start with a name?'

'Lauren Turner.' That was the easy part. The rest had to be mingled fact and invention. She gathered her forces. 'Age twenty-nine, with plenty of experience in childminding.'

'*This* child,' he returned, 'is thirteen. She lost her mother when she was eight. A particularly vulnerable age, I'm told. What she needs is someone young enough to be something of a companion for her over the summer, yet old enough and sensible enough to provide the proper care—with a little discipline thrown in for good measure. Late twenties sounds about right, if that's the truth. I'd have thought you younger.'

'It's the truth,' Lauren assured him. 'Flattered though I am by the assumption.'

The sudden grin was matched by the amusement sparkling his eyes. 'I'd doubt that. You strike me as far too level-headed to pay attention to flattery from any source. A good start, in fact, though I'd need a great deal more background detail before I could give you consideration.'

'Of course.' Lauren nerved herself to continue. 'My family moved to Canada when I was a teenager myself. I trained as a nanny when I finished school. I was with one family for five years looking after four children, followed by another two providing stand-in cover. For the last three years I've been with a Man Friday agency.'

Dark brows lifted. 'Man Friday?'

'Able to sort any problem. We—they can call on reliable, experienced help in just about every field. Saves busy people a whole lot of time and effort, *and* assures them of a good job.'

'A useful idea all round. Pity someone over here hasn't thought of it.'

'I'm sure they have. In the cities, at any rate. There probably wouldn't be quite the same call out here.'

'Maybe not.' He studied her once more, gaze shifting from her face to linger briefly on the thrust of her breasts beneath the close-fitting white top before moving on down the length of her legs and back again. 'You certainly look fit enough on it.'

The appraisement raised her hackles more than a little, but this was hardly the time to allow her sensitivities any sway. 'I am,' she declared. 'One hundred per cent!'

'More than many can claim.'

A statement almost certainly excluding himself, she reflected. There was no spare flesh on that frame of his, though more than a hint of muscle beneath the fine cotton shirt. A man who worked out pretty often, if she was any judge.

It took the fresh spark of amusement in the blue eyes to bring her back on track. She met his gaze squarely. 'What else can I tell you?'

He lifted one jeans-clad leg comfortably over the other, stretching the material taut across hard male thighs. 'Why have you returned to England?'

This, Lauren acknowledged, was where the lies really took over. The deeper she got the harder it was going to be, but she couldn't bring herself to back out now.

'I thought it time I sought my grass roots. Much as I love Canada, I'm still English through and through at heart.'

'You came back intending to stay?'

'For a year or two at least. I was taking a bit of a break before looking for a job, only it would be silly to pass up a chance like this. Always providing there is one, of course. Naturally, I'll understand if you feel otherwise.'

'Beggars,' he said, 'can't be too choosy. With an essential business trip scheduled for Monday, and my housekeeper refusing to accept any further responsibility, I'm in no position to look a gift-horse in the mouth. Maybe we should see how you and Kerry hit it off before we go any further though.'

He straightened his position to get to his feet. 'Sit tight while I go and find her. She's probably in the pool.'

Lauren let out a long sigh as the door closed in his

wake. The tension that had built over the last half-hour had her nerves stretched to their limits. There was every possibility that he'd still require some kind of reference before he made the final decision. A quick call now would prepare the way. Luckily she'd gone on the international tariff.

She got through to her former boss after some delay. With time at a premium, she went straight to the point. 'You'll probably be getting a call from a Mr Laxton asking for a reference. He'll need assurance that I'm a reliable, upstanding person.'

'You're all of that,' came the ready answer. 'Like I said before, you'd be welcome back any time.'

'I'll keep it in mind.' Lauren could hear the sound of movement from the hall. She added hastily, 'I have to go. Thanks, Bob.'

She slid the mobile back into her bag, heart going like a trip hammer as the semi-closed door was opened again by the man she was already up to her neck in deceiving. The girl accompanying him was wearing a towelling robe over a bathing suit, her feet clad in flip-flops. Tall for her age, dark blonde hair streaked by more than sunlight, she was merely pretty now, but showing signs of an emerging bone structure promising beauty to come. She gave no response to Lauren's wavery smile, hazel eyes devoid of expression.

'My daughter, Kerry,' said Brad. 'And this is Miss Turner. It is Miss?' he added.

'It is.' Emotions in turmoil, she somehow kept the smile going. 'Hello, Kerry. I'm Lauren.'

'Hi.' The tone was indifferent. 'Dad says you're from Canada.'

'I've lived there for some time, yes.'

'Do you ride?'

Lauren swallowed on the hard, aching lump in her throat, fighting to stay on top of the urge to reach out to the girl—the overwhelming desire to hold her close the way she had dreamed of doing these thirteen long years! Her voice sounded husky in her ears.

'I've done some. You have your own pony?'

'Horse. I'm past the pony stage. We have three. I'm going to get dressed. It's chilly in here.'

Lauren watched her walk out of the room, hunger unappeased. She hadn't been *that* sure of herself at twenty, much less thirteen! She had to have this job. She just had to! To be denied the only chance she was ever likely to have of spending time with her child was beyond contemplation.

It took everything she had to keep her face from reflecting the inner upheaval as she turned back to the man her daughter called father.

'So far, so good!' Brad Laxton commented. 'At least she didn't appear to take an instant slike to you. You've no objection, I take it, if I ring this company you were with in Canada for a reference?'

'None at all,' she assured him.

The number secured from her, he made the call right there and then. Lauren could feel his eyes on her as he waited for the connection to be made. She was only able to hear one side of the ensuing conversation, of course, but whatever was said, it appeared convincing enough. He'd obviously made up his mind by the time he put the phone down.

'You're staying at the Black Swan, right?'

'Right,' she confirmed. 'I only checked in a couple of hours ago.'

'So you didn't get round to unpacking yet?'

'No.'

'I'll have your bags fetched.' He paused, eyeing her quizzically. 'You didn't ask what the salary was.'

Lauren could have kicked herself. She did a hasty retrieval. 'I took it for granted it would be more than adequate in the circumstances.'

He laughed. 'On the grounds that I'm the one in most need? Fair comment. I'll make sure you're not disappointed. Anyway, I'll have you shown to the room you'll be using.'

Things were moving so fast Lauren could barely keep up. Two hours ago she'd been in possession of little more than a name and location, now here she was on the verge of becoming, if not exactly part of the family, in very close proximity to it. A move she would come to regret when the time came to leave, as it must, but that was six or seven weeks in the future.

The housekeeper was called to do the honours. In her mid-fifties and comfortably upholstered, the woman was introduced as Mrs Perriman. She greeted the news that Lauren was to join the household with unconcealed relief.

'You'll have your work cut out keeping that young lady out of mischief,' she said candidly on the way upstairs. 'Her father doesn't know the half of what she gets up to when she's home from boarding-school!'

'Is he often away?' Lauren asked.

'Often enough. Too many fingers in too many pies, that's my opinion. Not that he's anything but a good man to work for, mark you.'

'I understand you're none too keen on supervising Kerry yourself?'

'Well, I can hardly be expected to keep the whole place running smoothly *and* look after a teenager as well,' came the somewhat defensive answer. 'Especially one who likes her own way as much as Kerry does. She's been a long time without a mother.'

'Car accident, wasn't it?' Lauren murmured, riding the pang as best as she was able.

'Out and out murder, if you ask me! The culprit came round that corner like a bat out of hell just as she was drawing out of the gate. She was killed instantly, they said, and all he got was a fine and a ban.'

'It must have been a terrible time,' Lauren sympathised. 'For everyone.'

'It certainly knocked Mr Bradley back. Such a well-matched couple they were!'

'He hasn't contemplated marrying again?'

The older woman sniffed. 'If he hasn't, it isn't for lack of opportunity, believe me!'

Hardly surprising considering his assets, Lauren reflected. Physical, as well as financial, she had to admit. Not that she could afford to allow his undoubted masculine attraction to gain any kind of hold on her. That definitely wasn't what she was here for.

The room she was taken to lay along a side corridor leading from the west gallery. Larger than the living and sleeping areas of her apartment back in Toronto put together, with a carved four-poster bed as a focal point, it also boasted a well-appointed *en suite*.

Mrs Perriman left her to settle in, as she put it, saying she'd have her bags brought up the moment they arrived.

The window overlooked a wide stone balustraded terrace, from which steps led down to extensive lawns laid with flower beds, these in turn backed by woodland. Some distance away a latticed fence covered in clematis afforded a glimpse through of what Lauren took to be the swimming pool her employer had mentioned.

Turning back into the room, she stood for a moment in silent contemplation. Unlike on the ground floor, the carpets up here were fitted wall to wall. Incongruous with the period, perhaps, but offering a cosy comfort no hard floor could match. Especially in the winter months, she imagined.

The three watercolours on the walls were almost surely original works, although the signed name meant nothing to her. There would be little, if anything, in this house that wasn't the genuine article.

Apart from herself, came the rider. How long did she really think she could keep her secret when every instinct in her wanted to shout the truth from the rooftops? That was her daughter down there. Her baby! How did she keep *that* bottled up inside her?

There was a mirror on the wall opposite where she stood. Lauren studied her reflection, looking for points of resemblance. Apart from maybe the hair colour—making allowances for the streaking—and a certain something about the mouth, there was little as yet to tie the two of them together that she could see. Even less of the father, from what she could recall after all these years.

Her chest tightened as the memories came flooding back. The invitation to Roger Cosgrove's eighteenth birthday party had come as something of a surprise to start with as she'd given up hope of his noticing her. She'd pulled out all the stops to maintain his interest against all the competition, sinking every drink thrust on her in an effort to appear as worldly as the rest of them made themselves out to be.

She'd come to her senses far too late. Roger had denied everything, of course. It could have been anyone, he'd declared when her pregnancy was confirmed.

Lauren had wanted desperately to keep the baby regardless, but her parents wouldn't hear of it, and she hadn't possessed the courage to try going it alone. The child had been taken from her at just two days old to be handed over to the adoption agency. Six weeks after that the family had left for Canada and a new life.

A new life for *them*, but an unceasing heartache for *her*, she reflected painfully. There hadn't been one solitary day when she'd been able to put the memory aside completely. Moving to Canada hadn't helped in the slightest. If anything it had made things worse, because she hadn't even had old friends to fall back on.

The detective agency she'd hired to seek her daughter's whereabouts had managed it in a surprisingly short time. True, the detail they'd come up with regarding the kind of lifestyle her child was used to had proved a little daunting, but it hadn't cured her of the longing.

Her hope in returning to England had been just to catch a glimpse of the girl her baby had grown into. She hadn't even tried to think far beyond that. Standing here now, she was bound to acknowledge the lack of common sense in seeking this job. All it was scheduled to bring her was even more heartache.

In the eyes of the law, Kerry was Bradley Laxton's daughter. There was every possibility that she didn't even know she was adopted. Whether she did or not, the truth must stay hidden—for all their sakes.

Voices drifted up via the open window from the terrace below, one of them raised.

'I don't need looking after! I'm quite capable of doing that for myself! What do you really know about her, anyway?'

The reply was indistinct. Lauren went and closed the window, loath to hear any further protestations even while she could to a great extent understand them. Being left in the charge of anyone at thirteen would be galling enough, to be made answerable to a total stranger even more so. Breaking through that barrier was going to be far from easy.

She was still debating the best way to approach the problem when her bags were brought up by a middle-aged man whose weathered face suggested a lot of time spent outdoors.

'General factotum, miss,' he advised cheerfully when she asked what he did. 'John Batley. My wife works here too. One of the cleaners. Takes some keeping up to scratch, this place. Hear you're going to be keeping an eye on Miss Kerry.' He chuckled. 'Takes some handling, that one! Not that she's a bad kid at heart, just a bit uppity at times. Anyway, better get on. Mrs P said to tell you if you want tea later to just let her know. Mr Laxton doesn't usually bother.'

Lauren doubted if she would either, although it was probable that the evening meal would be served a great deal later than the six to six-thirty she was accustomed to back in Canada. Right now, food was of little importance.

Showered, and changed from the trousers and sleeveless top to a skirt and blouse in soft greens, she made her way somewhat tentatively downstairs again.

The house was quiet, the door of the room where Brad Laxton had interviewed her firmly closed. There were several other doors. The one she chose opened on a spacious drawing room panelled like the hall and superbly furnished. The grand piano standing under one window was probably one of the few items in the room less than a couple of hundred years old, Lauren judged.

She wondered if Kerry had inherited her own love of music.

The temptation proved too much. Going over, she sat down on the stool to open the lid on keys the colour of fine old ivory. The sound that emanated from her first soft touch made her quiver inwardly with delight. This was an instrument treated with all the loving care it merited.

Forgetting for the moment where she was, she began to play, choosing Chopin as befitting the mood of the moment. It had been some time since she'd last sat at a piano, and it took a minute or two for her fingers to regain their suppleness. As a child, she had entertained dreams of becoming a concert pianist some day, but had long ago learned to accept that her talent was limited. When she played at all it was for her own pleasure.

She was unaware of the door being pushed open again, until Brad Laxton spoke.

'My wife used to play that.'

Lauren's hands froze on the keys in guilty realisation. 'I'm so sorry,' she said. 'I had no right to touch it.'

'Apologies unnecessary,' he assured her. 'It was good to hear it again.' His smile was unexpectedly humorous. 'She'd have hellfire rained on me if I neglected to keep it maintained! You play well.'

'Thank you.' Lauren was finding his ease of manner difficult to react to. 'All the same, I should have asked permission first.'

His shrug made light of the comment. 'You must treat the place as your home while you're here. No restrictions. You might even encourage Kerry to take it up seriously again. She hasn't shown all that much interest since she lost her mother.'

'Understandable, if they used to play together.'

Lauren did her best to keep her tone level. 'I can try, but she might not appreciate it.'

'Possibly. She's more for outdoor pursuits these days. How are you at tennis?'

'I know one end of a racket from the other.'

The grin was appealing. 'I've a feeling you'll hold your own whatever the challenge. I was about to have a drink on the terrace. Feel like joining me?'

Lauren closed down the piano lid. 'Why not?' she said lightly.

He hadn't moved from the doorway. Moving towards him, she felt like an insect pinned to a board for dissection under the unwavering blue gaze. While he might appear benevolent enough on the surface, she had no doubt that he'd prove a formidable opponent when crossed. Should he discover her secret there would be hell to pay for certain. Only he wasn't going to discover it. No one was.

'You look pensive,' he observed as she reached him. 'Worried about something?'

'Not at all,' she lied. 'Will Kerry be joining us?'

'Depends how long she's out with Diamond.' He turned back into the hall alongside her, tall, lean and disturbingly close. 'How well can you ride?'

'I've never fallen off,' she said truthfully, not about to admit how comparatively limited her experience in that particular sport was. 'You said Kerry plays tennis too. Do you have your own court?'

'We do. You can't see it from the house.'

'Did you never think of moving somewhere smaller?' Lauren ventured.

'After Claire died, you mean?' He shook his head. 'She loved this place. So do I. So does Kerry. It might be a bit impractical for the two of us, but it's home.'

With memories he didn't want to let go of, she assumed. It was apparent that he'd loved his wife a great deal. Enough to perhaps make the thought of replacing her with someone else anathema to him.

It was still extremely warm outside. The late-afternoon sun gave a lovely golden glow to the landscape, highlighting the massed azalea bushes at the far end of the lawns. Seated beneath a wide cream shade, Lauren sipped the orange juice she'd asked for and tried to think of something—anything—to say.

She was very much aware of the man seated opposite. No woman with normal reflexes could fail to be aware of him. Looks, wealth, vital good health, he had it all!

Except for the wife he had loved and lost, came the reminder.

'Why aren't you married?'

Coming out of the blue, the question jerked her head up as if she'd been stung. It took her a moment to gather herself.

'No one ever asked me.'

'Looking the way you do, I find that hard to believe.'

'It takes more than looks.'

'True, but you're certainly not lacking in personality. Or is it that Canadian men prefer their women more subservient?'

Lauren had to smile at the idea. 'If they did, they'd be sadly disappointed.'

'Just a thought.' Brad was smiling too. 'You should give it a try. Marriage, I mean. Maybe get some kids of your own instead of looking out for other people's. The clock might not tick as hard and fast as it used to for a woman, but there's a limit to how long it ticks for.'

'I'll bear it in mind,' she said on a somewhat cooler note. 'Did you never want more children yourself?'

'Unfortunately, my wife was unable to have any at all.' His tone was calm, the blue eyes steady. 'Kerry is adopted.'

It took Lauren every ounce of control she had to keep her own tone from reflecting her state of mind. 'I'm sorry again, Mr Laxton. That was a very personal question.'

'But something you should probably be aware of. And the name is Brad.'

Lauren inclined her head in recognition, still struggling to keep her emotions under wraps. 'Does Kerry know?'

'We told her when she was five. It doesn't appear to have affected her in any way, though I imagine she sometimes wonders about her real parents.'

'But she's never suggested trying to find them?'

'Not up to now. Hopefully never. They gave up all rights when they placed her for adoption.'

'There might not have been any choice.'

'There's always a choice. Not always the will. Still, without people like that there'd be no chance for those unable to produce a child for themselves, so I can't be too hard on them.'

Hard enough, Lauren thought hollowly. If he knew the truth, his opinion of her as a fit person to take care of *any* child would undergo an abrupt alteration.

'You're looking pensive again,' he remarked.

She shook herself. 'A touch of homesickness, that's all. It's all so different here.'

'You said you'd lived in Canada some years?'

'Long enough to have grown accustomed to the pace of life out there.'

'I trust the homesickness isn't going to affect our arrangement?'

'I've no intention of letting it,' she said. 'What I start, I finish.'

'My sentiments exactly.' He sounded relaxed again. 'I'll have to remember to thank George for suggesting the job might suit you.'

'He didn't exactly suggest it,' Lauren admitted. 'I overheard him telling someone about it, and just took it from there.'

'A lucky break for us both, then.'

Kerry appeared as if from out of the blue, taking a seat without a word. She was wearing the clothing in which she'd obviously been riding, and smelled quite strongly of horses. Lauren made an attempt to draw her out.

'Good ride?'

'Diamond is always a good ride,' came the short response. 'She needs an experienced hand, though, so you'd probably find her too much for you.'

'Oh, I don't know.' Lauren kept her voice light. 'I'll give anything a try.'

A spark leapt in the hazel eyes. 'I bet you wouldn't get up on Caliph!'

'No, she wouldn't,' her father stated firmly. 'You'd better not attempt it again either. It takes a stronger hand than yours to hold him in check when he takes a mind to do a runner. Lauren can use Jasper.'

Kerry looked far from happy at the suggestion, though she made no further comment. Jasper had probably been Claire's horse, Lauren reflected.

'How long might you be away?' she asked Brad, looking for a change of subject.

'Depends how things go,' he said. 'A week tops.'

'I could have come with you,' said Kerry. 'I wouldn't have minded being on my own during the day.'

'In New York?' Brad laughed, shaking his head. 'I don't think so! Anyway, you'll have Lauren for company. I'm sure the two of you can find plenty to occupy your time.'

'We'll certainly do our best,' Lauren agreed. 'You might like to show me something of the area,' she added to Kerry.

'The car you came in?' Brad queried before his daughter could answer. 'Hired?'

'Well…yes.' Until this moment, Lauren hadn't given it a thought.

'Assuming you don't want to be landed with a vast bill, it would be an idea to turn it in. Which company did you use?'

'Hertz,' she said.

'We can drop it in Stratford, then. There's a couple of cars here you can choose from. Do you prefer manual or automatic?'

Lauren shook her head, doing her best to take it all in her stride. 'I really don't mind. What about insurance?'

'We'll take care of that too tomorrow.' He glanced at his watch. 'I'll have to leave you to it. I've a couple of calls to make. See you at dinner if not before.'

Two pairs of eyes watched him stride off indoors. Kerry was the first to break the silence.

'Don't think you're going to get *your* hooks into Dad!'

Taken totally aback, Lauren was a moment or two finding a response. 'Have others tried?'

'Lots. They're always fawning round him!' There

was venom in the young voice. 'Dad's happy the way he is. He doesn't want another wife!'

Lauren forced herself to say it. 'Any more than you'd want another mother. That's understandable. You must miss her terribly.'

Whatever reaction Kerry had been expecting, this obviously wasn't it. She looked a little confused. 'Is your mother dead too?' she asked.

'No—but I do know what it's like to lose someone you love. No one can replace them.' Lauren paused again, searching for the right note. 'I've no designs on your father, Kerry. I'm here to do what I'm being paid to do, and that's all.' She lightened her tone deliberately. 'It's a job in a million, I have to admit.'

A gleam sprang in the girl's eyes. 'I wouldn't count on it!'

'You mean you'll do your best to see me off?' Lauren smiled and shook her head. 'I'm not easily gotten rid of.'

'We'll see.' Kerry got to her feet, defiance evident in every line of her supple young body. 'I don't need looking after, by you or anyone! I can take care of myself!'

Lauren watched her stalk off. Uppity, John Batley had called her. She was all of that. But then what might be expected of a child deprived as she had been of a mother's influence at such a vital age, with a father who seemed to think more about business than his daughter's well-being?

Her daughter, she thought with sudden fierceness. *Her* responsibility—for the next few weeks, at any rate. However tough leaving her at the end of it would be, it couldn't be any worse than the total deprivation she'd suffered up to now. At least she'd have some memories to fall back on.

CHAPTER TWO

WITH no clear idea of what time dinner might be, she went to find Mrs Perriman and ask.

Mr Bradley liked to eat around seven-thirty when he was home, the woman advised. Nothing formal. There hadn't been a proper dinner party at Ravella since the mistress had died.

'You'll be eating with him and Miss Kerry, of course,' she said.

It hadn't occurred to Lauren to think anything else. 'Perhaps we could have the meal at six-thirty while Mr Laxton's away,' she ventured. 'If that's all right with you?'

'It certainly is. It will give me a nice long evening.' The older woman looked well pleased. 'You and I are going to get on, I can see.'

Hopefully so were she and Kerry, once she'd got through to her that she'd no interest whatsoever in becoming the next Mrs Laxton, Lauren thought. It wouldn't be an overnight transformation for certain.

She spent what was left of the afternoon exploring part of the landscaped grounds. The full-sized tennis court lay down a path beyond the swimming pool, surrounded by eight-foot-high wire netting. A fairly recent addition, Lauren judged. Recently used too, if the racket left lying on the bench at the rear was anything to go by.

On impulse, she went through the gate to collect it,

wielding it in her hand for a moment. It was too light for a man, so it had to be Kerry's. Careless of her to leave such an expensive item out to warp in the sun. But then there was little incentive to take care of things when replacements were probably forthcoming for the asking.

She took it back to the house with her, laying it on a table in the hall where it couldn't fail to be seen. If she was to give Kerry a game, she would have to borrow a racket for herself, but there were sure to be spares.

Brad emerged from the study as she headed for the stairs.

'There you are,' he said. 'I've been looking for you.'

'I thought I'd take a walk to get my bearings,' Lauren explained a little guiltily. 'I've no idea where Kerry got to.'

'You're not expected to spend every waking moment with her,' he returned. 'Especially on your first day. She's probably in her room plotting to make life as difficult as she can for you.'

Lauren allowed herself a smile. 'She can try.'

'That's the spirit!' he applauded, sobering again to add, 'I'm under no illusions about her behaviour this last year or so. She seems to go out of her way to alienate people. You're closer to your teen years than I am. Do you recall being like that?'

'Not exactly.' Lauren hesitated, aware of treading on tricky ground. 'Though I might have been in Kerry's circumstances.'

Blue eyes pierced her through. 'You think her neglected?'

'In the sense that she sees so little of you, perhaps. I realise you've a lot of commitments, but…'

'But?' he prompted as she paused again.

'You could possibly arrange matters so you're around more during the school holidays.'

'Unfortunately, things don't work out as neatly as that.' Brad's expression was contained, but there was a definite chill to his voice. 'Or maybe I should take retirement and devote my whole life to her.'

'That wasn't what I meant,' she protested.

'But you don't approve of boarding-schools.'

Lauren set her chin, not about to back down now. 'Generally speaking, no. They're no substitute for a home environment. Bringing in a full-time carer might have been a better option.'

'A pity I didn't have the benefit of your advice five years ago.'

'Isn't it!' She regretted the snappy retort the moment the words left her lips. 'I apologise,' she said quickly. 'It isn't my place to criticise.'

'No, it isn't,' he agreed. 'Don't make me regret taking you on.'

He turned back into the room from which he had just emerged, closing the door on her. Lauren stood for a moment biting her lip in recognition of having overstepped the mark. She'd hardly been here five minutes, for heaven's sake! It was going to take every bit of diplomacy she could summon to retrieve the situation. If she could retrieve it at all.

Reluctant though she was to face him again, hunger alone was incentive enough to drive her downstairs at quarter past seven. Only on reaching the hall did she realise that she had no idea where the dining room was. There was so much of the house she hadn't seen as yet.

She was still standing there dithering when Brad appeared. He had jettisoned the jeans in favour of finely tailored trousers and a thin silk sweater. There was no telling what his thoughts might be from his expression.

'There's time for a drink before we eat,' he said. He opened a door on the right. 'In here.'

Lauren went through ahead of him to a comfortable sitting room bathed in evening sunlight. Only half the size of the drawing room, it boasted an inglenook fireplace and oak beams.

'Ravella's a bit of a hodge-podge of styles, as you see,' Brad declared, crossing to a cabinet against the far wall. 'Too many owners with different ideas over the years. What will you have?'

'Gin and lime, please,' Lauren requested, opting for the first thing to come to mind. She watched him pour the drink, calling on her reserves to make the first move. 'Mr Laxton—' she began.

'I told you to call me Brad,' he said.

'Brad, then.' She paused uncomfortably. 'About this afternoon—'

'Forget it.' He turned to bring the glass across to where she'd taken a seat in one of the cretonne-covered chairs, the gaze he rested on her face devoid of animosity. 'If I flew off the handle it was only because you hit a raw spot. I took the easy way out sending Kerry off to boarding-school, I admit. It just seemed the best thing all round at the time.'

Lauren kept her voice steady. 'Did the fact that she was only an adopted daughter have any bearing, do you think?'

'No.' It was said with certainty. 'I might not have been as desperate for a child as Claire was in the beginning, but I was captivated the moment I set eyes on

Kerry. She was just one month old when we got her—
as pretty as a picture even then.' His voice was reminiscent. 'Claire was in her seventh heaven! We tried for
another, but nothing came of it. A disappointment from
all points of view. Kerry would have loved a brother or
sister.'

Lauren swallowed hard on the tightness in her throat.
'You could marry again.'

'In order to maybe provide her with one?' He
shrugged. 'I'm thirty-nine. The patter of little feet
doesn't hold quite the same appeal any more.'

'There are other reasons for marrying.'

'To give her a mother, you mean? I doubt if she'd
welcome any substitute.' His mouth tilted. 'Or were you
thinking more of *my* needs?'

Lauren held his gaze squarely. 'I shouldn't imagine
you have any difficulty whatsoever in fulfilling those.'

He laughed. 'You don't pull your punches, do you?
Outspoken as they come!'

'I never saw any advantage in beating about the
bush,' she returned. 'Not that it hasn't got me into trouble a time or two.'

'I can imagine.' He studied her a moment, taking in
every detail of her face within the bell of wheaten hair,
his brows drawing together a fraction. 'There's no
chance we've ever met before, is there?'

Lauren drew a steadying breath. 'I'm sure not. I'd
have remembered.'

The strong mouth curved again. 'I'll take that as a
compliment.' He finished his drink in one swallow.
'Anyway, we'd best go on through before Mrs P gets a
huff on.'

Having barely started her own drink, and disinclined

to finish it quickly, Lauren left the glass where it was on the small table beside her chair. She still felt churned up inside from that moment back there. While she couldn't see all that much resemblance between Kerry and herself, it seemed that he might have picked up on some element of familiarity without realising the source.

Even if he did eventually realise it, the likelihood of his guessing the truth was too remote to be of concern, she assured herself. There was no such thing as a totally unique set of features.

Dinner proved something of a trial, with Kerry refusing to answer Lauren's overtures in anything but monosyllables. Brad's patience finally ran out when she shoved a sauce boat across at Lauren's request with such force that its contents splashed across the cloth.

'That's enough!' he clipped. 'If you can't be civil, leave the table!'

Face mutinous, the girl got to her feet and stalked from the room with a dignity Lauren could only admire. She stayed silent with an effort, but her expression gave her away.

'You disapprove.' It was a statement not a question.

'I think you were a bit harsh,' she confirmed. 'I'm going to have difficulty reaching her at all if you come the heavy father.'

'So what would you have had me do?' he demanded. 'Ignore it?'

'No, just perhaps temper the way you react to it a little. I'd be willing to bet you hadn't even told her you were looking for someone to take charge of her for the summer before this afternoon.'

'You'd be right,' he admitted. 'I saw no point when it might not even happen.'

Lauren looked at him curiously. 'Just what *would* you have done if I hadn't turned up?'

Broad shoulders lifted. 'Relied on Mrs P taking on the mantle as usual, I suppose.'

'That would have come dangerously close to emotional blackmail.'

'I know.' The grin was disarming. 'I make no claim to angel status.'

'But you certainly wouldn't have considered delaying your overseas trip?'

'As I already told you, it isn't that easy. It's taken a lot of time and effort to get this deal on the table. Delay isn't on the cards.'

The housekeeper's return to the room put paid to the reply forming on Lauren's lips. The former eyed Kerry's unfinished plate in some obvious annoyance.

'You can take it away,' Brad told her. 'She won't be back.'

Whatever the woman's thoughts, she was keeping them to herself. Brad poured more wine for the two of them as she departed, sitting back, glass in hand, to view Lauren with lifted brows. 'Do we spend the rest of the meal debating my failings as a father?'

The question brought her up short. She'd done little but criticise since she'd got here, she realised. There was no doubt of his regard for Kerry, and she had to admit that the girl's behaviour just now had been a little over the top. So perhaps she wouldn't have reacted quite so strongly herself if one of her former charges had expressed themselves in similar fashion, but she was trained in child management. It was maybe time she started making a few allowances.

'I'm sorry,' she said. 'I'm overreacting myself. I know how difficult young teenagers can be.'

'Tell me about it,' he said humorously. 'You're going to have your work cut out this next week, but I've every faith in you.'

'Thanks.' Lauren kept her tone light. 'That's quite an accolade on a few hours' acquaintance.'

'I'm a good judge of character, if nothing else,' he returned equally lightly.

'Oh, I think as one of the leading industrialists in the western hemisphere you can claim to be rather more than just that!'

The dark brows rose again. 'You seem to have done some homework on me.'

'You've been featured by the Canadian media,' she said hastily, aware of being on the verge of revealing a little too much knowledge of his background.

'My fame goeth before me!'

'I didn't connect the name right away, if you're thinking what I think you might be,' she claimed on an edgy note. 'It was the job that attracted me, not the possibility of...'

'Of?' Brad prompted as she came to an abrupt stop. There was a deep-down sparkle of laughter in the blue eyes. 'Securing yourself a rich husband?'

Lauren had to smile herself. 'Some might have it in mind.'

'If you were one of them, you'd be concentrating on gaining favour rather than hauling me over the coals.'

'Unless I was perceptive enough to realise a yes woman would bore you into the ground.'

He grinned. 'That's certainly true. Maybe I'm not so good a judge of character after all.'

'Yes, you are,' she said, abandoning the flippancy. 'I'm here for Kerry, nothing else. Are you going to let her go the whole night without food?'

'If you're thinking of suggesting she's invited back, she wouldn't come,' he returned. 'Mrs P will see to it that she doesn't starve.'

Lauren let it go at that. There'd be time enough to try breaking through the shell her daughter had donned against her.

They had coffee on the terrace. The air was balmy, the layer of light cloud across the western sky already tinged with colour from the lowering sun. A faint breeze wafted in myriad scents.

A lifestyle just about anyone would give their eye-teeth for, Lauren reflected, looking out over the lovely landscape. All this for one man and one child! Not that either of them spent all that much time here, from what she could gather. Kerry would be in school two thirds of the year, Brad probably out of the country as often as he was in it.

'Moonlight becomes you,' murmured the latter, dragging her out of her reverie.

'There isn't any moonlight yet,' she pointed out.

'I know.' His smile taunted. 'But it got your attention.'

'I imagine you're unaccustomed to having to claim it,' she returned. 'According to Kerry, you have women falling over themselves to be with you.'

'Kerry exaggerates. She even suspects a friend's eighteen-year-old daughter of having designs on me.'

'But not the other way round?'

He quirked an eyebrow. 'I prefer mature women. Around your age, say.'

She'd asked for that, Lauren acknowledged. 'I was out of line,' she conceded.

'You make a regular habit of it,' he said. 'I think you must like living dangerously.'

Green eyes widened. '*Am* I living dangerously?'

The smile was slow. 'Oh, yes!'

Lauren caught herself up in the realisation that she was flirting with the man. Hardly a wise move considering the conversation they'd just had over dinner, jesting though that had been. There was no denying the effect he had on her though. Sitting there now, broad of shoulder and deep of chest, the pushed-up sleeves of his sweater revealing a light covering of dark hair over muscular forearms, he exuded masculinity in a way that sent her pulses into overdrive.

'I believe I just caught another glimpse of the real Lauren Turner under that cool and collected guise,' Brad observed.

'A momentary aberration,' she claimed, recovering her poise outwardly if not inwardly. 'It won't happen again.'

'A pity.'

He was silent for a moment, studying her—raising her pulse rate even further. When he spoke again the banter was missing.

'There's a lot more to you than meets the eye—easy though you are on it. You're not in some kind of trouble by any chance?'

Lauren felt her heart give a painful jerk. 'What would make you think that?'

He gave a brief shrug. 'Just a feeling.'

'Intuition?' she suggested, opting for a chaffing note.

'I thought we women were supposed have cornered the market.'

His mouth creased. 'Meaning the average male is far too dense to be sensitive to underlying currents?'

'It's one way of putting it. I'd say being of a more pragmatic bent. I haven't robbed any banks, so you can rest easy on that score. I did park in a disabled space once though, come to think of it. Maybe it's delayed guilt that's coming through.'

Brad was laughing now, holding up his hands in surrender. 'I should know better than to try plumbing a woman's mind!'

'As if we're anything but the most straightforward of creatures!' she declared, drawing a breath of relief that the danger point was past. Not that he could possibly have guessed the real reason for whatever constraint he'd sensed in her.

'That I'd definitely argue with,' he said. 'I suppose it's all part of the charm, never knowing quite what may be going on inside those lovely heads.'

'It cuts both ways,' she returned, matching his tone.

'Not nearly to the same extent.' He was leaning back in the chair again, vivid eyes sparkling in the light from the setting sun. 'Right now, I'm an open book.'

He was too: enough so to start a slow curl in the very pit of her stomach. She hadn't been without male friends over the years, but none of them had made her feel the way he was making her feel right now. The way he'd made her feel the moment he opened the door to her this afternoon, if she was honest about it. The antagonism had been more by way of defence than anything. If it weren't for Kerry...

If it weren't for Kerry, she wouldn't be here to start

with, came the reminder. *She* had to be her only concern.

'I think it's time I turned in,' she said.

'Running away?' he taunted as she pushed back her chair to get to her feet.

'In need of a good night's sleep,' she countered. 'It's been a long day.'

His shrug was philosophical. 'There's always tomorrow.'

There were a whole lot of tomorrows, Lauren reflected, making her way indoors. She'd need to keep an extremely tight rein on the emotions Brad roused in her if she was to last the course without creating even more problems than she already had on her plate. He'd made it more than obvious tonight that he found her an equal draw.

At least he'd be gone for several days. That would give her time to get a grip on herself.

Surprisingly, considering her state of mind, she slept well after some initial tossing and turning, awakening at seven to another sun-filled morning.

They were to take the car into Stratford to turn it in, she remembered while dressing. Hopefully, Kerry could be persuaded to come along too.

Breakfast was being served on the terrace. She found Brad alone, a newspaper opened before him. He looked up to greet her with an expression devoid of anything but solicitous enquiry.

'Restful night?'

Lauren matched his tone, determined to keep a lid on her responses. 'Perfect, thanks.' She took a seat, reaching for the coffee-pot standing on a heated mat. 'Kerry not down yet?'

'Kerry,' he said, 'was up and out on Diamond before seven. She's in the pool at present, taking advantage of the weather while she has the chance. You should do it yourself. It's due to break.'

'Back to normal, then,' Lauren commented. 'For England, anyway. Apart from the occasional storm, we can usually rely on three to four months of summer in Toronto.'

'How do you normally spend the summer?' he asked. 'Your leisure time, at any rate.'

'The usual ways. Sports, barbecues, et cetera. I have a friend who owns a small yacht.'

'Male?'

'No.' Lauren refused to meet his gaze. 'I'm not in a relationship.'

'There's such a thing as a platonic one.'

This time she did glance his way, unsurprised to see the taunting light in the blue eyes. 'You really reckon?' she asked sarcastically.

He grinned. 'For some, maybe. I don't see all that many men thinking nothing but pure thoughts where you're concerned. You're not built for it.'

Mrs Perriman's emergence from the house with a fresh rack of toast closed the conversation, if it could be called that. Lauren refused the housekeeper's offer to cook her something, happy to settle for the toast and marmalade. Accustomed as she was to alfresco eating during evenings and weekends, breakfast was usually taken on the run. Gracious living certainly had its high points.

Brad had returned to his newspaper. A stranger might

even take them for a long-married couple, Lauren reflected with a cynical edge. She studied the bronzed features, dwelling for several pulse-quickening moments on the sensual line of his mouth. She could imagine the feel of it moving against hers, soft and slow at first, mounting gradually to passion; the hardness of the muscular body as he moulded her to him; the strength in his arms as he lifted her up to carry her…

She came down to earth with a bang at the realisation that she was under scrutiny herself. Brad watched the warm colour flood her cheeks with interest.

'At the risk of inviting another snub, I'd say you were thinking much the same thing I spent most of the night thinking about,' he observed. 'It isn't often I'm kept awake.'

'I'd doubt you suffer frustration very often,' she retorted, gathering herself. 'Most women would be only too glad to accommodate you.'

'Contrary to the impression you seem to have developed of me, I'm not interested in *most* women,' he returned. 'You're very different from the general run.'

'Because I don't give out on less than twenty-four hours' acquaintance?'

Dark brows quirked. 'Meaning you might consider it after two o'clock this afternoon?'

'No.' She had to smile herself. 'I might find you attractive—all right, *do* find you attractive,' she amended as the mobile left eyebrow lifted once more. 'But that's as far as I'm prepared to go. Today, or any other day. What time do you propose leaving for Stratford?'

'When you've finished,' he said. 'No particular rush.'

His easy acceptance of the change of subject left her

feeling somewhat demoralised. A ridiculous reaction considering what she'd just finished telling him.

The truth being, she hadn't meant a word of it, she acknowledged wryly.

'Will Kerry be coming too?' she asked, striving to hit a level note.

'I doubt if she'll want to. Not that we'll be gone that long, anyway. I have things to do. I'll be free after lunch though,' he added. 'We can all three of us take a ride together.'

He'd naturally want to judge her ability for himself, Lauren realised with some trepidation. She'd done a reasonable amount of riding, if only on stable hacks. Providing Jasper had no temperamental traits, she'd probably manage OK.

'I'll look forward to it,' she lied.

Kerry came up the steps at the far end of the terrace, dripping water from beneath the towel wrapped around her. Her hair was soaking too, the lighter blonde streaks darkened by the water. Lauren wondered how and when she had acquired the streaks. It was almost certainly not with Brad's authority.

'How's the water?' she greeted the girl smilingly.

'It's heated,' came the short reply. She reached for a piece of toast, spreading butter thickly and marmalade even more so.

'Didn't you have breakfast?' asked her father as she took an overlarge bite from the slice.

'I'm making up for missing most of dinner last night,' she said pointedly. 'I don't have the weight to lose.'

His lips twitched. 'Let's hope you don't have to miss any more meals, then. How do you feel about going riding this afternoon?'

'The two of us?'

'The three of us,' he corrected. 'Lauren needs to get acquainted with Jasper.'

The animation that had lit the young features went into swift decline. 'I suppose,' she said.

'We're going to Stratford to turn in my car this morning,' Lauren put in. 'Why don't you come too?'

'No, thanks,' came the stony reply.

She dumped what remained of the toast on a plate, and continued on into the house. Blue eyes met green across the width of the table in resigned recognition of the censure expressed there.

'Now what?'

'You might have asked her yourself,' Lauren returned.

'I'd have got the same answer.'

'You can't know that for sure.'

'I do, believe me. When she gets that look on her face there's no shifting her.' He folded the newspaper. 'You might find you've taken on a harder task than you imagined.'

Lauren lightened her tone, aware of being drawn into unfair criticism again. 'I'll survive.'

'I hope so. I wouldn't want to find you gone when I get back.'

There was no taunt in his voice now—nor in the blue eyes holding hers. Lauren felt her inner thighs go into involuntary spasm. Would it really hurt to indulge a physical need for once in her life? she asked herself yearningly. Others did it all the time.

Except that this was no common situation, the man she was contemplating becoming intimate with was no one-night stand she could simply walk away from.

There was so much more to him than that. *Too* much! It was going to be hard enough saying goodbye to her daughter when the six weeks were up. Falling for Brad was the last thing she needed.

She wrenched her gaze away and got to her feet. 'I'll go and collect the paperwork for the car.'

There was no sign of Kerry when she got indoors. Not that it was likely she'd have been persuaded into coming along, anyway. The afternoon's ride was hardly scheduled to improve matters either, once it was realised how far from expert a rider she was—especially in comparison with Claire. It was wrong, Lauren knew, to be jealous of the woman who had given her child the love she'd been unable to give her, but it would take a saint not to be.

CHAPTER THREE

BRAD was leaning against a silver Alpha Romeo parked alongside her hired Ford saloon when she got outside again. The close-fitting cords he was wearing emphasised the narrowness of waist and hip opposed to his breadth of shoulder.

Why couldn't he have turned out to be short and fat and balding? she thought with rueful humour.

It was a ten-mile drive into Stratford. Brad led the way, sticking to a meritous thirty-five along the winding, hedge-bound lanes until they reached the wider road leading directly into the town.

Concentrating on following the silver car through the traffic-thronged streets, Lauren gained only an overall impression of the place. It was obviously very different from what it would have been in Shakespeare's day, but certainly worth another visit.

She was glad to reach the hire company's offices and turn in the car. They proved a little reluctant to take a drop-off without prior arrangement, but Brad sorted things out with them. From there, they went to arrange insurance.

They were on their way back to where they'd left the Alpha when Lauren almost got run down by a car driven by some maniac running the traffic lights. Brad yanked her out of the way with bare seconds to spare.

'Blasted idiot!' he swore. 'Did the wing mirror catch you?'

Lauren moved her head in the negative. She was vitally aware of the hand still curving her upper arm, of the look of concern in the blue eyes. 'I'm fine,' she said. 'Thanks to you. I never saw it coming.'

'People who drive like that should be locked up and the key thrown away!' he declared roughly.

He'd lost his wife through a driver like that, Lauren reminded herself. Small wonder he felt so strongly about it.

'You look shaken up,' he said. 'I think a few minutes sitting down with a coffee would be a good idea.'

The near miss hadn't affected her nearly as much as his touch was doing; she could feel the tingle right through her body. So much for keeping a tight rein on her responses!

'It really isn't necessary,' she assured him. 'I'm fine.'

He ignored the protest, drawing her with him as he headed towards the river.

They went to a café backing on to the water, securing a garden table just vacated. Lauren watched a narrow boat chugging upriver at the regulation four miles an hour while they waited for the coffee to arrive, admiring the artistry in the brightly painted exterior.

'That must be a nice, restful way to spend a holiday,' she commented.

'Not quite so restful on the canals when there are locks to be navigated,' Brad rejoined. 'There's one section on the Grand Union with fourteen in a row. It takes a whole day to get through.'

Lauren brought her attention back to the hard-boned features, riding the impact. 'You've done it yourself?'

'Once,' he confirmed. 'Claire fancied trying it when we first moved out here. She stuck it for three days before deciding it wasn't for her.'

'Was Kerry with you?'

'Yes. Having to keep a constant eye on her didn't help, I suppose. Those boats aren't all that safe where young children are concerned.'

'I imagine not.' Lauren hesitated before taking the plunge. 'I can appreciate how hard it must have been for you when you lost Claire, but were there no grandparents to help out?'

'Claire grew up in an orphanage herself,' he returned unemotionally. 'My parents divorced many years ago and lead their own lives in different parts of the world.'

Lauren bit her lip. 'I'm sorry.'

'No need. It was a fair enough question. And before you ask, I could have afforded to rest on my laurels by then—the problem being that I wouldn't have been worth living with. I need challenge in my life.' The pause was brief, the change of tone meaningful. 'One kind or another.'

'Don't start *that* again,' she said shortly. 'I already told you...'

'I know what you told me. The same thing I've tried telling myself, with just as little effect.' He added softly, 'I want you, Lauren. And don't try bringing in the time element again. I felt this way the moment I clapped eyes on you.'

'Are you always as quick off the mark?' she asked after a moment.

'You don't listen, do you?' he said. 'I told you at breakfast I'm no profligate.'

'You'll be telling me next that I'm the only woman who's aroused your interest in years!'

'I'm no liar either,' he returned equably. 'There's been no one serious since Claire died. If I haven't married again it isn't through loyalty to her. She'd have been the last person to want me to spend my life in mourning. She'd have liked you. You have quite a lot in common with her.'

Lauren felt her heart jerk. 'Such as?' she murmured.

He smiled. 'Will-power, for instance. It took a lot to change her mind once she'd set it.'

'But you usually succeeded.'

'Not always. It made for some battles at times—me liking *my* own way so much too.'

Lauren couldn't help but respond to the humour in his eyes. 'I'll bet! I imagine she was very beautiful.'

'On the assumption that I couldn't possibly be attracted by anything less?' He viewed her judiciously, taking in every vibrant feature of her face beneath the sun-kissed cascade of her hair. 'You're actually quite right, though true beauty's in the eye of the beholder. I loved her very deeply.'

Lauren had all on to keep her emotions from surfacing. She'd never been loved like that. Not even by her own parents, who had always made it clear that she'd been an accident they could have done quite well without—especially after she got herself pregnant. They'd moved from Toronto to the west coast some years ago, leaving her to the life she'd forged for herself. She visited once a year, more for the look of it than through any real feeling. Without the latter, blood was no thicker than water.

'It's gone ten-thirty,' she said hollowly. 'Shouldn't we be heading back?'

There was a certain speculation in his regard, but he made no further comment.

With the weekend traffic at saturation level, it was well gone eleven when they finally made it back to Ravella. Brad departed at once for the study, leaving Lauren to wander outside in search of Kerry.

She found her daughter sunbathing on a lounger at the side of the blue-tiled pool, her tender young curves covered only by the bottom half of a brief bikini.

'I hope you've used plenty of sun cream,' Lauren commented, reining back on the instinctive protest.

'Why should *you* care?' the girl demanded without lifting her head. 'I'm just an excuse for you to be here!'

'You're the *only* reason for my being here,' Lauren assured her. 'I want us to be friends, Kerry.'

'Is that what you want Dad to be too?'

'Your father's my employer. It isn't quite the same.'

'Oh, I'll bet it isn't!' The sarcasm crackled. 'You're no different from the rest! You're all of you just after his money!'

Lauren took a seat on the edge of the lounger next to her before answering, her tone mild. 'Generally speaking, I'd say he has rather more to offer than just that.'

'Only you're not interested in any of it, of course!'

'That's right. I'll be leaving when you go back to school.'

'Why don't you go now?'

'Because I've no intention of quitting a good job.'

There was a momentary pause, a slight change of tone. 'That's all it is to you?'

'At the moment, yes. Whether it comes to mean any more is largely up to you. As I said, Kerry, I'd like us to become friends.'

The blonde head swivelled, hazel eyes regarding her with scepticism. 'What use would there be in that if you're going away again?'

'Six enjoyable weeks as opposed to six miserable ones?' Lauren suggested. 'We could have a lot of fun together.'

'You're too old to have fun with,' came the scathing retort.

'Try me,' Lauren invited.

It was almost possible to hear the cogs turning in the younger brain as the offer was considered. Kerry came up on her elbow, her sudden smile innocent as the day. 'All right, so come for a swim for starters. We never have lunch before one.'

Undeceived, but not about to pass up even the slightest chance of making a breakthrough, Lauren nodded. 'Good idea. I'll go and change.'

She got to her feet to skirt the end of the lounger. Unprepared for the shove in the centre of her back—though she probably should have been—she teetered on the pool edge for a heart-thudding second or two before gravity overcame balance, propelling her into the water.

Dressed the way she was in light cotton trousers and top, there was little drag. She surfaced without spluttering, having managed to take a breath, treading water to push the hair from her eyes as she looked up at the girl standing on the pool edge.

'Not quite what I had in mind,' she said, gathering herself, 'but now I'm in I may as well stay in. Aren't you going to join me?'

Whatever reaction Kerry had been expecting, this obviously wasn't it. She looked totally nonplussed.

'I suppose you're going to tell Dad I pushed you in,' she said in an attempt to recapture her former belligerence.

'I don't see any reason to,' Lauren returned equably. 'How about a race? I warn you, I'm pretty fast though.'

The challenge had the desired effect. Kerry jumped straight into the water. 'You're on!' she declared.

They started from the end, both using the crawl.

Hampered by the clinging material, Lauren found some difficulty in keeping pace with the girl at her side, much less drawing ahead. Kerry was first to touch the rail, turning in laughing triumph.

'I win!'

'Only because I was handicapped by a certain person,' Lauren responded, laughing back. 'You wait till next time!'

'I'll still beat you!' Eyes sparkling, face alight, Kerry looked so different from the moody teenager of the morning. 'I'm in the school team!'

'So was I. I trialled for the Olympics.'

'You did?' Kerry looked really impressed. 'Did you get a medal?'

'No, I didn't make the team.' Lauren watched the animation slowly fade from her daughter's face in wry acknowledgement of her mistake in bringing the subject up. There was no kudos in failure. 'Have you thought about going for it yourself?' she added lightly. 'You certainly have the makings.'

'You won't flatter me into liking you,' came the short reply.

She heaved herself from the pool, stamping across to seize the towel she'd been lying on a few minutes before. Lauren swam back to dive for the sandals she'd dropped off before beginning the race, ruefully aware that she had a long way to go before she got anywhere near the girl. It was dangerous to get *too* close, she knew, but that didn't stop her from wanting to. Just to see her look the way she had a few minutes ago made it all worthwhile.

Kerry was lying on her front again, face turned away in pointed dismissal, when she emerged from the pool. Lauren resisted the temptation to try another approach right now. At least she'd proved it was possible to get through the barriers, if only fleetingly.

She gave herself a rub-down with a towel to remove the worst of the drips before heading for the house, sneaking in via a side door with the intention of finding a route to her room that didn't involve using the main staircase.

It was odds on that she'd run into someone, of course. Mrs Perriman regarded her bedraggled appearance in astonishment.

'What on earth happened to you?' she exclaimed.

Lauren pulled a rueful face. 'I slipped on the poolside. I thought this the best way to come in rather than drip water all over the place.'

'Slipped, you say?' It was obvious that the other didn't believe a word of it. 'You'd better take the back stairs. That young lady needs a good smacking!' she added severely as Lauren headed down the indicated corridor.

What the young lady in question needed most was a mother, Lauren reflected, wishing it were only possible to take up the role herself. Brad did his best, but in all fairness, he could hardly be expected to give up everything he'd worked for in order to spend his life bored half out of his mind. Even if he did remarry, there was no guarantee that it would be to someone capable of giving Kerry the mother love she'd missed so much these past five years.

She managed to find her room without too much trouble. Her wet clothing left hanging over the bath-side to dry off, she put on fresh underwear and a plain white cotton dress. Even with the help of a hair-dryer, it took time to restore order to the heavy length. By the time she finished it was almost one o'clock.

Apart from a splash of lipstick, she didn't bother with make-up. She wasn't, she told herself forcibly, out to impress anyone.

With the weather still holding out, lunch was served on the terrace too. Lauren was last to make the table. Her own hair fully dried and neatly brushed, Kerry regarded her with a hint of defiance.

'I hear you had a dip in the pool,' said Brad as she took a seat. 'Enjoy it, did you?'

There was no innuendo that Lauren could define in his tone. Regardless, she played it straight. 'Very much in this heat. I'd have thought an open-air pool a bit of a white elephant generally though.'

'If it's kept heated, it's even pleasant in the rain. We don't use it in the winter,' he added drily. 'That might be going just a bit *too* far.'

'I'm sure.' Lauren avoided eye contact with Kerry. 'There have to be limits.' She paused. 'Did you get done what you wanted to do?'

'Most of it. I'm still up for a ride, if that's what you're thinking about. Providing you've something more practical to wear, that is?'

'I've got jeans,' she said. 'And some walking shoes that should do. I don't have a hat though.'

Brad gave her an assessing look. 'I think I might find you one that will fit.'

Kerry opened her mouth as if about to make some comment, closing it abruptly as he glanced her way. She looked mutinous again.

Changing for the ride later, Lauren regretted the lack of proper gear. Jeans were considered standard riding garb where she came from, but she doubted if many people in this neck of the woods would hold the same view. If she was going to do this on a regular basis, she would have to do something about getting kitted out.

She found Brad on the terrace. He looked impressive in the pale beige jodhpurs and shining brown leather boots.

'You'll do,' he greeted her. 'Have you visited the stables yet?'

'No, I've only been as far as the tennis court,' she said. 'There's a lot of ground to cover.'

'Right, then, it's this way. Kerry went on ahead.'

They dropped down the far end of the terrace to cross the lawns and follow a path through the narrow neck of woodland. Too vibrantly conscious of his closeness, Lauren found herself unusually tongue-tied. She could feel the heat from his body, the tingling brush of his bare arm against hers.

'Something bugging you?' he asked.

'Should there be?' she said.

Brad gave her a swift sideways glance. 'There's something very irritating about being asked a question in answer to a question.'

'I know.' She made an effort to get herself back on an even keel. 'I'm a bit concerned about this ride, if you must know. I'm not really all that experienced.'

'You won't have any problem with Jasper,' he promised. 'At fourteen, he's lost a lot of the high spirits he had when Claire rode him. You'll soon pick up. Kerry will see to that. She's been riding since she was three.'

Lauren felt the familiar lump rise in her throat. She'd missed so much! 'I bet she looked really cute,' she murmured.

'She certainly did. Proud as a peacock in all the regalia. There'll be a photograph somewhere. Claire filled many an album. You'll have to get Kerry to find them for you.'

They emerged from the trees on a cobbled yard bordered by the stone-built stable block. Kerry was already astride her own bay mare.

'I was beginning to think you'd found something better to do,' she said tartly.

'There couldn't *be* anything better,' Lauren chipped in before Brad could answer. She studied the two waiting animals. 'Which is Jasper?'

Kerry gave a disgusted snort. Lauren couldn't blame her. Considering the grey was a full stallion, the question had been a pretty stupid one. The chestnut gelding stood considerably higher than the sturdy trekking ponies she was used to. She had to take Brad's word for it that he was reasonably docile.

The hat fetched from the tack room for her by the young man who appeared to be in charge of the stables proved a good fit. It seemed unlikely, after five years, that it had been Claire's, though Kerry's reaction to the offer earlier seemed to point that way. She had little choice but to wear it, anyway, until she got one of her own.

Brad gave her a leg-up into a saddle half the size of the American version. She felt decidedly insecure. He swung himself lithely onto the grey, holding the horse in check as it pulled at the bit.

'Lead on,' he said to Kerry. 'We'll go up by the burrows.'

She moved the mare ahead, at one with her mount in a way Lauren could only envy. They were both of them so totally at home in the saddle. The way Claire would have been too. She could imagine them out like this as a family group, although Claire was still a hazy figure in her mind's eye. Blonde, brunette, redhead? She had no idea.

Her confidence increased as they traversed the narrow lane, with Jasper proving to be the steady ride she'd been promised. Kerry opened a field gate without dismounting, holding it for the other two to come through, and making sure it was securely fastened again.

'OK?' asked Brad, pulling into step beside Lauren as they headed up the sloping field.

'Fine,' she assured him. She patted the gleaming neck. 'He's a good ride!'

'You have a good seat,' he said.

'No more than yours,' she riposted. She urged Jasper ahead to the sound of his laugh, gaining in confidence by the second. It was exhilarating to be out here like this, the sun on her face, the smell of horse and leather mingled in her nostrils, the smooth movement of silken muscles between her thighs. She could live this life forever!

Brad caught her up, grinning at the sparkling look she turned on him.

'I told you you'd be OK on Jasper. You can let him go when you're ready.'

In tune as she felt with this horse, she could really enjoy a gallop, she told herself recklessly.

The view from the top of the hill was superb: a rolling vista of green and gold, with the mellow stone of the village lying a mile or so away no intrusion on the scene. From here, it was possible to see Ravella in its entirety, standing proud amidst the landscaped grounds. Impractical it might be for a family of two, but Lauren could well understand Brad's reluctance to let go of the place.

'Ready?' he asked, curbing an impatient Caliph, and she took a deep breath.

'Let's go!'

Kerry had already gone, slim young body glued to the saddle, hair flying out from under her hat. Jasper followed Caliph straight into a gallop without any urging, causing Lauren an instant of terror swiftly erased by even greater exhilaration as she settled to the rhythm. Easy as pie! she crowed as they ate up the track. Impossible to fall off if she tried!

She should have remembered the old adage. The rabbit that darted from the tall grass bare inches in front brought the gelding to a sudden snorting stop. Totally unprepared, Lauren found herself propelled forward over his head to slide to the ground in an ungainly heap.

Brad was off his mount and back to where she lay almost before she could draw breath.

'Are you hurt?' he asked in genuine concern.

'Only my pride,' she acknowledged ruefully, sitting up. 'Brought down to earth by a rabbit!'

'It could happen to anybody,' he assured her.

Not to him, she thought. He'd always be in total control. She took the proffered hand to be drawn to her feet, unable to hide a grimace as pain shot through her shoulder.

'Just bruised a bit, I expect,' she asserted before Brad could say anything. 'It could be worse.'

'A whole lot worse,' he agreed. 'You could have broken your neck!' He laid a hand on the bruised shoulder, pressing gently along the line of the bone. 'Seems intact. Try moving your arm.'

She did so, this time keeping her expression from reflecting anything at all. His touch, like this morning, was creating havoc. He knew it too. She could see it in his eyes, in his slow smile.

'I want you,' he said softly.

Heart going like the clappers, she turned away to look for Jasper. He was side by side with Caliph, the two of them taking advantage of the stop to make a meal of the succulent grass. Some yards further on, Kerry sat astride Diamond, her expression a study in conflicting emotions.

'You can't even ride properly, can you?' she accused. 'Mom never fell off a horse in her life!'

Lauren put a hand on Brad's arm as he started to speak. 'I'm sure she didn't,' she said. 'I'll obviously never come near the same standard, but you could teach me the finer points of horsemanship.'

'Somebody had better,' came the short, sharp answer. 'While Jasper still has a leg to stand on!'

Lauren turned a rueful look on Brad as Kerry wheeled Diamond about and cantered away. 'Would you call that progress?'

'I'd call it downright rudeness,' he said. 'You should have let me—'

'It would have done more harm than good if you'd told her off. Anyway, she was right. I put Jasper at risk by not being in proper control.'

'The best of us can be thrown by the unexpected.' Brad bent to plant a swift kiss on her lips, smiling at her expression. '*Ergo!* Do you feel like continuing, or would you rather head for home?'

The best way of dealing with the incident was to ignore it, Lauren decided, although it was going to be difficult with her mouth still retaining the impression the way it was. Damn the man! she thought wryly. Didn't she have enough on her plate?

'Either way, I have to get back up there,' she said.

'So we'll take it slowly from here.'

He went to fetch Jasper out of the grass, holding him for her to mount. She pulled herself up with some slight difficulty due to the ache in her shoulder, taking up the reins again with a sense of make or break.

Kerry was still in view up ahead, cantering along the ridge.

'Don't you ever worry about her when she's out on her own?' Lauren couldn't help asking.

'To a certain extent,' Brad acknowledged. 'I could come the heavy and stop her riding alone, but she'd hate me for it.'

'I doubt it. I doubt if there's anything you could do that she'd hate you for. She thinks the world of you.'

He slanted an ironic glance. 'Even though I neglect her so badly?'

'I was unfair,' she admitted. 'You're a long way from being the worst father I've come across.'

'That's something of a comfort. How does the shoulder feel now?'

'It aches a bit.' Lauren was glad of the change of subject.

'You're probably going to have quite a bruise,' he observed. 'I'll find you some liniment.'

Kerry had turned to head back towards them. She slowed Diamond to a walk as she came up, looking a little discomfited.

'I shouldn't have said what I did,' she muttered. 'It wasn't your fault Jasper shied.'

She was off again before Lauren could respond, this time at a full gallop.

'Now that definitely *is* progress,' Brad commented

drily. 'At this rate, you'll be the firmest of friends by the time I get back.'

Lauren had doubts about that. It was certainly a start though.

Cloud had been growing from the west over the last hour. By the time they reached the stables it had spread to cover a good half of the sky.

'The forecast was rain on the way,' Brad observed as he slid the saddle from the grey back. 'Lucky we got this in when we did.'

'*I'm* not afraid of getting wet,' claimed Kerry. The glance she shot Lauren was lacking in belligerence, if not exactly warm. 'I don't suppose you'll be all that eager to take Jasper out in the rain.'

'I can think of a lot worse things,' Lauren returned mildly. 'I might even join you early morning tomorrow. Providing you'll have me, of course.'

Slim shoulders lifted. 'If you like.'

Brad raised a quizzical eyebrow as she headed for the tack room with her saddle. 'Another breakthrough!'

'Maybe.' Lauren was still not counting any chickens, uplifted though she felt. 'We'll see how it goes.'

The rain started on the way to the house. Just a drop or two at first, then as if the heavens had opened. They ran the last few yards, gaining shelter before they got more than slightly damp.

'There goes the summer!' Brad remarked.

'I bet it won't be raining in New York,' said Kerry.

'If it is, I probably shan't know about it. I'll be cooped up indoors most of the time.'

Lauren said lightly, 'We'll be thinking of you working your fingers to the bone while we enjoy ourselves here, won't we, Kerry?'

'Doing what?' asked the latter.

'Whatever we fancy on the day.'

The hazel eyes acquired a faint spark of interest. '*I* fancy taking a boat on the river. A big one!'

Lauren got in before Brad could open his mouth to make the anticipated response. 'The biggest!'

Brad gave her a bland smile. 'Sounds a nice idea. Let's hope for a return of the heatwave. You two go on up. I've a phone call to make.'

Kerry's room turned out to be only a couple of doors down from the one Lauren was occupying.

'I'm surprised I didn't hear you going past this morning,' she said on realising.

'The doors are too thick to hear anything through them,' came the response. 'You'll have to set your alarm if you do want to come with me in the morning. I'm always up by half-past six.'

'No problem,' Lauren assured her. 'I'll be ready and waiting.'

She went on into her room feeling immeasurably cheered by the lessening of hostility. It might not happen overnight, but she'd get there in the end.

She refused to listen to the part of her mind that asked: *and then what?*

CHAPTER FOUR

IT TURNED out to be just the two of them at dinner. Mr Bradley had gone out, Mrs Perriman advised. No, he hadn't said where he was going, she told Kerry.

'I bet he's gone to see Diane!' exclaimed the latter disgruntledly.

Lauren aimed for a casual note. 'Who's Diane?'

'Some woman. I heard him talking to her on the phone yesterday.'

'You haven't met her yourself, then?'

'No, and I don't want to!'

'Your father's entitled to friends,' Lauren chided gently. 'Even women friends. It doesn't mean he's planning on getting married again. Although, do you really think your mother would have wanted him to be on his own for the rest of his life?'

'He isn't on his own,' came the stinging retort. 'He has me!'

'Only part of the time. And what about when you grow up, maybe go away to university?'

'That won't be for years!'

'Not that many.' There was a pause while Lauren searched her mind for the right words. 'Your father loves you very much, Kerry, but you have to understand—'

'He isn't my real father.' The statement was flat. 'I'm adopted.'

'I know.' Lauren could have bitten her tongue off for

the over-hasty response, seeing hostility spring in the hazel eyes again.

'He told you!'

'Not in any depreciative sense. Parents having children naturally have to take what they're given. You were chosen.'

It didn't need the expression on her daughter's face to underline the triteness in what she'd just said. The response was biting.

'I wasn't chosen, I was available. My real parents didn't want me.'

'That's not…' Lauren broke off, catching her lip between her teeth. 'Not necessarily true,' she amended. 'They probably just thought it better for you to be with someone able to give you the things they couldn't, that's all.'

'Would *you* do that?'

The question hit with all the force of a blow to the solar plexus. It took Lauren everything she had to keep her voice from reflecting her inner turmoil. 'I certainly wouldn't want to, but a child's welfare has to come first. It's possible your mother—your real mother—was very young, and just wasn't able to cope with bringing up a baby.'

Kerry's brows drew together. 'You mean, she might not even have been married?'

Lauren hadn't meant to go down that road, but it was too late to backtrack now. 'Whether she was or not, I'm sure she loved you a great deal.'

There was a lengthy silence. Kerry toyed with her fork. When she did speak again it was expressionlessly. 'One of the other girls at school is adopted too. She's met *her* real mother.'

Lauren found herself holding her breath. 'How did she get on with her?' she managed.

'She said it was horrible! There were two boys they said were her brothers!'

'Half-brothers.' Lauren was doing her best to stay on top of a situation she herself had instigated. 'It can't have been easy for anyone.'

'Well, it won't happen to me!' The tone was suddenly fierce. 'I *never* want to meet *my* real mother. She gave me away!'

The lump in Lauren's throat was threatening to choke her. She swallowed thickly, wishing she'd never begun this. She ached to tell her how sorry she was; to tell her how much she loved her and had always loved her. Only she couldn't do that. She couldn't do anything but sit there and take it.

Finding other topics of conversation didn't prove easy. Kerry disappeared right after the meal, leaving Lauren to contemplate a lonely couple of hours before she could reasonably think about bed.

There was every possibility that Brad would be spending the night with his lady friend. He had a perfect right to do that, of course, but he'd get short shrift if he tried coming on to *her* again. He was good at it, she had to admit. In less than twenty-four hours, he'd had her closer than she'd ever been to acting on the intense physical attraction between them. It just went to show what a gullible fool she still was.

She wandered outside until dusk, coming back indoors to stand irresolute in the hall for a moment or two, before giving in to the urge to play the piano. As Kerry had said, the doors in the house were too thick for sound to carry far, so she wouldn't be disturbing anyone.

The music soothed her as always. She lost herself over the next hour, working her way through every piece she could remember, then trying out some new ones from the pile of sheet music she found in the piano stool.

It was even more of a shock this time when Brad came into the room, because she hadn't known he was back.

'Don't stop,' he said.

She already had, although she didn't get up from the instrument. 'I didn't realise you were home,' she said expressionlessly. 'Or that the sound would travel through the door.'

'It didn't. I heard it through the window as I drew up.' His voice was reminiscent. 'Like old times.'

He sank to a seat in a nearby chair, laying his head back against the cushion. 'Play some more, will you? I feel in need of a little soothing.'

Lauren obeyed, resisting the impulse to just get up and go. Wearing a superbly cut suit in dark grey, shirt pristine white, he looked more businessman than beau, but maybe that was how his date liked to see him: the powerful magnate!

'Did you have a good evening?' she asked.

'As good as it gets,' came the somewhat ambiguous answer. His eyes were closed, legs comfortably stretched, his whole attitude one of relaxation. 'Sorry to walk out on you like that. I hope Kerry continued to behave herself.'

Lauren kept her voice soft. 'She was no trouble at all.'

'Really?' He sounded a little sceptical. 'Mrs P said she caught you creeping in dripping wet before lunch. Do you usually go swimming fully clothed?'

'I slipped,' she said.

'Not what Mrs P seems to think.'

'She wasn't there.'

'And you've no intention of telling tales out of school.' The blue eyes were opened now, the expression in them hard to define. 'You'd bend over backwards rather than drop Kerry in it, wouldn't you?'

'If necessary,' she agreed.

Still playing, she eased the shoulder she had fallen on that afternoon. It was going to be painful by morning as the bruising started to come out. That early ride could be a real challenge—providing Kerry hadn't changed her mind after tonight's set-back.

Her pulse leapt as Brad got up and came over to stand behind her, laying his hand along her collar-bone to gently massage it as he had done earlier. She could see the two of them reflected in the uncurtained window. The expression on his face as he looked down at her left little doubt of what was in his mind.

She closed down the piano lid, fingers unusually clumsy. 'I'd better turn in if I'm going to make that ride in the morning. I doubt if Kerry will wait if I'm not there on the dot.'

'I'd doubt it too.' Brad had moved back a step to allow her to get up from the stool. 'An early night won't do me any harm either.'

It was only half-past ten, Lauren realised, glancing at her watch. She'd thought it much later. She stiffened as a fingertip stroked the nape of her neck where the hair had parted.

'Don't!' she got out.

'I can't help it,' he said softly. 'You've been driving me up the wall, one way or another, since you got here.' He turned her about, the smile on his lips echoed in his eyes as he searched her face feature by feature. 'I want you, Lauren!'

'So you keep telling me.' She pulled away from him. 'I'm going to bed. Alone, if you're in any doubt.'

'Oh, for such strength of mind!' he murmured.

'Don't pull that one on me,' she retorted. 'You're no more unable to keep control of your urges than I am!'

The smile grew. 'So you do admit to having them?'

Striving to keep a level head, she sought refuge in sarcasm. 'I dare say we all have them. It's what we do about them that counts. If you've spent a frustrating evening, tough, but don't look to me for relief!'

A line appeared between the dark brows. 'What makes you think I might have spent a frustrating evening?'

'I... You were back so early,' she floundered, already regretting the untimely remark.

'And where exactly do you think I've been?'

Lauren hesitated, but saw no way out of it. 'Kerry thought you'd probably gone to see someone called Diane.'

'She was right, as it happens—though I don't know how she got the name. We had dinner together, then I dropped her off at her home. With no intention of anything else, so you can forget the frustration theory.'

Lauren spread her hands in a helpless little gesture. 'I'm sorry.'

'No need.' If he was angry at all, it wasn't showing. 'Did I detect a certain element of jealousy, by any chance?'

'No, you didn't,' she denied, a little too swiftly for conviction. 'I've no reason to be jealous. I've—'

'I know. You've no interest in anything or anyone but Kerry. Keep repeating it often enough and you might convince yourself.' He put both hands to her face, forcing her to look directly into his eyes. 'But you won't convince me,' he added softly. 'You want the same thing I want, Lauren.'

The tremors running through her were a give-away in themselves. She closed her eyes when he kissed her, savouring the feel and taste of his lips.

It was just as she'd imagined it, the movement slow and gentle, almost playful at first. He slid his hands round to cup the back of her head, fingers tangling in her hair, petalling her lips apart with his silky, infinitely sensitive tongue.

Lauren heard his roughened exclamation as she moulded instinctively to his hardened masculine shape. His hands moved again, this time dropping the length of her back to cup the firm curves of her behind and draw her even closer. His mouth was an endless source of pleasure, carving a slow passage down the taut line of her throat to linger for tantalising moments at the vulnerable hollow before pressing onwards to seek the shadowed cleavage revealed by the low-cut V of her close-fitting top.

'You've too many clothes on,' he murmured against her skin. 'We've both too many clothes on!'

And they were staying on, she thought achingly, dragging herself back from the brink while she still retained some small degree of sanity. She was teetering on the edge of far more than just physical involvement with this man. Something she dared not allow herself.

Brad made no attempt to stop her as she twisted away from him, just stood there looking at her with an expression that made her wince.

'I didn't have you down for a tease,' he said.

'I'm not.' She struggled against the urge to throw

herself back into his arms and take whatever she could of him. Her voice shook a little. 'I just don't think it's a good idea, that's all.'

'That wasn't the impression you were giving a moment ago.'

'I know.' She made a wry gesture. 'You're a very... persuasive man, Brad. I got carried away.'

There was a certain cynicism in the line of his mouth. 'That makes two of us. I'll keep a tighter rein on my urges.' He made an abrupt move towards the door. 'Have a good night.'

There was, Lauren conceded ruefully, little more to be said. She'd rejected him—end of story. From now on, he'd leave her alone.

There was a hollowness in that thought.

A restless night and subsequent late awakening put paid to the planned ride. Both father and daughter had finished breakfast and gone about other pursuits by the time Lauren got downstairs.

Mrs Perriman accepted her apologies with good grace, quite prepared to cook her a full breakfast if she wanted it.

'Have you any idea where Kerry is?' Lauren asked, perching on a kitchen stool to eat the toast she'd settled for.

'She's gone to play tennis, I think,' answered the housekeeper.

'On her own?'

'There's one of those ball-machine things. She uses that when there's no one around to give her a game.'

'Her father doesn't play, then?'

'Oh, yes. Whenever he has the time.' The woman gave her a shrewd look. 'Attractive, isn't he?'

Lauren did her best to look amused by the question. 'I suppose he is.'

'There's no suppose about it. There isn't a woman in the district wouldn't fall over themselves if he beckoned!'

'Even the married ones?' Lauren asked blandly, prompting a chuckle.

'One or two I could think of. Not that he would. He's too much sense to get himself involved in that kind of thing. Do you have a boyfriend?' she added.

Lauren shook her head. 'Not in England. Not a serious one anywhere, in fact,' she tagged on lightly. 'I'm heart whole and fancy free, as the saying goes.'

'I'll bet there's been no shortage of lads after you though, looking the way you do. You've never wanted to settle down—have some children of your own?'

'It would be nice, but I haven't met anyone I'd want to settle down with,' Lauren answered on as level a note as she could manage. 'I'm happy doing what I do.'

'Not forever, though, surely? What about when you're older? Being on your own isn't good, believe me. I was only forty-five when I lost my husband, and we'd no children. If it weren't for getting taken on here at Ravella, I don't know what I'd have done! You mark my words, you'll regret it if you leave it too late.'

'I think I'd regret it even more if I got married just for companionship in my old age,' Lauren said mildly. 'You obviously loved your husband a great deal.'

'I did, yes. He was a good man.' There was a pause, a change of tone. 'It's time Mr Bradley started thinking about the future too. Kerry will be leading her own life in a few years. You could do a lot worse.'

Lauren almost choked on the coffee she'd just raised

to her lips. 'Are you suggesting what I think you're suggesting?' she got out.

The older woman looked unperturbed. 'It's worth thinking about, isn't it? I've seen the way he looks at you—*and* the way you look at him.'

'I do not!' Lauren allowed herself a faint smile, seeing the twinkle in the other eyes. 'I think you're misreading things a little.'

'Oh, I don't know. Lust's a good start.' The twinkle grew at the look of shock on Lauren's face. 'I may be getting on a bit, but my memory's still good. Your generation didn't invent sex, you know.

'Anyway, you'll not mind if I leave you?' she tagged on, voice briskening. 'I need to tell the cleaners to concentrate on the east wing this morning.'

She bustled off, leaving Lauren to review the conversation they'd just had in some bemusement. Never judge a book by its cover, she told herself. Mrs P had hidden depths!

The suggestion was a definite non-starter though. It wasn't a wife Brad was out for.

She took her time over breakfast, not looking forward to coming face to face with him again after last night. There was every likelihood that her rejection was the first he'd ever had to deal with. His ego would have taken quite a battering.

She was being unfair again, and she knew it. She hadn't exactly discouraged his advances. Allowing herself to fall hook, line and sinker for the established father of the daughter she could never claim as her own would be sheer folly. She was already too dangerously close to it.

The sky was clouded over today, but it was dry and still very warm. Breakfast finished, she made her way out to the tennis court to seek her daughter, nonplussed on reaching it to find her already involved in a game with Brad.

Her first inclination was to turn tail and leave them to it, but she'd already been spotted. She stayed to watch instead.

Hips lean, thighs hard-muscled, Brad looked superbly fit in the white shorts and T-shirt. Despite her youth, Kerry was giving him a far from easy time of it. Enjoying every minute too, the laughter bubbling from her lips as he failed to reach a well-placed shot.

'I win that one!' she crowed.

'Sheer luck,' he returned. 'I'm way out of practice!'

He turned to head for the side-bench and the towel lying there, lifting a sardonic eyebrow at Lauren standing the other side of the fence.

'If it's a game you've come for, you're hardly dressed for it.'

'I thought I'd ask Kerry first if she wanted one,' she returned levelly. She directed a smile at the girl watching the two of them with some disfavour. 'Her standard of play's very high for her age.'

'Are we going to play again?' Kerry called across.

Towel slung about his neck, Brad turned back to her, shaking his head. 'I've had it for now. Lauren will give you a game though.'

Face set, she lofted a ball and smashed it across the court. 'I'll use the machine, thanks.'

'Just don't forget to put the cover back when you've finished,' he said.

Lauren chewed on her lip as Kerry went to pull the ball machine out from its corner and into position. Things had improved before the talk about adoption last night, but it was back to square one this morning, it seemed. Trying again would probably be a complete waste of time and breath for the present. Once Brad was out of the way, she could concentrate all her attention on the girl.

Brad caught up before she reached the end of the shrubbery, falling into step at her side.

'I take it you're staying on?' he said.

'I hadn't actually thought about leaving,' she admitted. 'Would you prefer me to go?'

'Because I failed to get you into bed last night?' He gave a brief shrug. 'All part of life's pattern. I came on too strong too fast. My mistake.'

'If it's any consolation, it was one of the hardest decisions I've ever made,' she confessed. 'I just didn't think it a wise move, that's all.'

'So you said.' He slanted a glance, taking in the wry tilt to her lips. 'I'm still not sure why. We're two adult people with the same basic urges. What's so wrong with indulging them?'

'Nothing normally, I suppose.'

'So it's the situation here you're worried about? You reckon we're neither of us entitled to consider our own needs?'

'You are, I'm not.' She tried to sound matter-of-fact about it. 'I'm just staff, in effect.'

'And never the twain shall meet? That idea went out with the Victorians.'

'So I'm an old-fashioned girl,' she murmured, drawing a sudden grin.

'Shaped like one, I'll admit.'

'You just can't help it, can you?' Lauren accused.

'Seems not,' he agreed. 'A reprobate of the first order!' He nodded approvingly at the involuntary smile. 'That's better.'

'You're being very…jocular about it all,' she said after a moment. 'Most men wouldn't be.'

'I'm not most men,' he returned.

Lauren could go along with that. She'd certainly never met another like him.

'What time do you leave tomorrow?' she asked, thinking how much she was going to miss him.

'Right after breakfast. I've a flight at two-fifty, into JFK around five-thirty. Half-past ten here, of course. Tuesday we get started.'

'You really enjoy it, don't you?' she said, hearing the lift in his voice.

'Enjoy might not be quite the word.'

'Thrive on it, then.'

'I suppose I do. Life would be pretty tame without it.' Brad gave her another sideways glance. 'As I've said before, I need challenge. How's the shoulder to-day?'

'It aches a bit,' she acknowledged. 'Nothing radical.'

'Bad enough to keep you from riding this morning though.'

'I overslept.' She pulled a face. 'I imagine Kerry was pretty scathing about it.'

'She didn't make it either, it seems. I've no idea why,' he added before she could voice the question. 'She didn't volunteer an explanation, and I didn't ask.' He paused briefly. 'The liniment would still help.'

'Thanks. I'll use it tonight before I go to bed.'

'Best to start right away. You can come and collect it now, if you like.'

It was Lauren's turn to shoot a glance. 'From your room?'

'Bathroom actually, but you can stay near the outer

door if you think my passions might get the better of me.'

What she felt at the moment was gauche. 'I really don't see you in that light,' she said diffidently.

'That's a relief.'

Lauren had the sense to let the subject lie. What she couldn't do was control the responses his very presence was drawing from her. She could feel the radiated warmth, catch the faint tang of a healthy male body recently exerted. However much she might fight it, she still wanted him desperately.

His bedroom opened off the west gallery. Overlooking the front of the house, it was large enough to hold a sitting area in addition to the double bed with its carved head and footboards and heavy wardrobes. An essentially masculine room, the carpet and drapes a deep, warm gold against panelled walls, the sofa and chairs covered in a practical brown fabric.

Brad disappeared into the *en suite* bathroom, emerging moments later with a bottle in his hand.

'There's enough here for several applications,' he said. 'Are you going to be able to manage without help?'

It was going to be difficult reaching the main area of bruising, Lauren knew, but accepting his aid would be too much like putting her head in the lion's mouth. 'I'll cope,' she said.

There was derision in the blue eyes. 'Still having doubts about my ability to control those urges?'

'I didn't have them to start with,' she denied.

'Prove it,' he challenged. 'Liniment needs massaging in for it to penetrate properly.'

He had her there, Lauren admitted. If she refused to let him do it, she was as good as saying she didn't trust him. What she trusted a great deal less was her own restraint.

'Well?' he prompted. 'Do I get the job, or don't I?'

Her shrug was as casual as she could make it. 'Thanks for the offer. It would be better, I suppose.'

'Right.' He indicated the doorway he'd just emerged from. 'Through here.'

Lauren followed him into the spacious bathroom, too intent on keeping her butterflies caged to pay much attention to surroundings.

'I can't get to it with your shirt on,' he said when she took a seat on the stool he drew forward.

Logical, if not something she'd thought of up to this minute, Lauren conceded reluctantly. She slipped the buttons, easing the material down from her shoulders— too vitally conscious of the looming male presence at her back. 'Will that do?'

'You'll need to slip your bra strap down a bit too,' he said. 'That's one hell of a bruise you've got!'

Lauren obeyed again, refraining from covering the exposed upper curve of her breast with her hand. He was simply using the situation as a means of proving she had nothing more to worry about from him.

Pouring a little of the liniment into his palm, he set to work. The first touch of those long, tensile fingers sent a tremor right through her. He couldn't help but feel it himself, although he made no comment. She knew from a look in the mirror this morning that the bruising covered a larger area than she'd imagined. She suspected it was probably going to get worse before it got better. Lucky it was her left shoulder that was affected, not her right. At least she could still manage a game of tennis if and when the opportunity arose.

Her attempt to take her mind off the supple movement of those hands wasn't working. The thudding in her ears was getting faster, heavier as the blood heated in her veins, the tension in her stomach spreading downwards, spasming her thigh muscles. She had a yearning to lean back against the hard body—to feel him slide his hands down beneath her bra to caress the aching flesh.

She jerked upright as he did exactly that. 'You promised!' she got out.

'I lied,' he said. 'Tell me you want me to stop and I will.'

There wasn't a cat in hell's chance of her raising that amount of will-power again, and he knew it. Lauren couldn't even have found the breath to say the words. She relaxed instead, leaning back against him as she'd wanted to do, head tilting as he bent to put his lips to the tender, sensitive spot behind her ear. Floating on cloud nine, she was totally devastated when Brad withdrew his hands and lifted her bra strap back into place, unable for a moment or two to think straight.

'Payback, was it?' she managed as he moved across to replace the liniment in a mirror-fronted cabinet.

'Just testing the water,' he said, washing his hands at the basin. 'I'm not giving up on you, Lauren. You don't really want me to. You just proved that.'

She buttoned up her shirt with fingers that were all thumbs, face burning. 'The only thing I proved was that *you* can't be trusted to keep your word!'

He turned back from the basin, towel in hand, a smile hovering about his lips. 'I told you I like a challenge.'

'And I'm telling you you're a louse!' she shot back.

'Temper!' he admonished. 'Why don't you admit the truth? You enjoyed that as much as I did.'

'It's nothing to do with enjoyment, it's to do with

integrity,' she said with what dignity she could muster. 'Something you obviously wouldn't know anything about!'

'That comes dangerously close to slander. I could put the company lawyers on to you.'

'It's not the company I'm talking about! It's you, you...'

She gave up, unable to maintain the tirade in the face of the grin creasing his lips. Her smile was reluctant. 'All right, you made your point.'

'What point would that be exactly?'

'That I'm lacking in moral fibre myself, when it comes down to it.'

'There's nothing immoral about two people being drawn to one another. The shoulder feel any better?'

The abrupt change of subject made her blink. She hadn't given her shoulder a thought in the last few minutes.

'I...think so,' she said, flexing it.

'Then I'll see you later. I need a shower,' he added. 'A cold one!'

He wasn't on his own, she could have told him. He'd had steam coming out of her ears just now. She was sorely tempted to abandon discretion and offer to join him.

She left him to it, pausing outside the bedroom door to gather herself. Common sense advised steering well clear of any further involvement in what could only be a temporary affair at best. By the time Brad returned from his trip, she had to have herself in hand. Things were going to be hard enough as it was.

CHAPTER FIVE

RELUCTANT to be around when he emerged from the shower, and conscious of the job she was supposed to be doing, she went looking for Kerry, only to find the tennis court deserted, the ball machine left uncovered.

Lauren pushed it back into the corner, and replaced the waterproof cover, wondering where else to look. The stables was as good a place as any to start, she supposed.

Finding a path that seemed to lead in the right direction saved her from retracing her steps. Her guess proved right. Kerry was chatting animatedly with the youth who took care of the stables. She looked thoroughly disgruntled on seeing her.

'What now?' she demanded.

'Nothing in particular,' Lauren answered mildly. 'I was just taking a walk.' She switched her attention to the young man still leaning nonchalantly against the tack-room door. 'Hello again! Mick, isn't it?'

'Hi!' he said, not attempting to move. 'I've been hearing all about you.'

Face flushing, Kerry shot him a reproachful glance. Lauren smiled pleasantly. 'That's nice. Were you planning on going riding, Kerry?'

'Obviously not right now.' The truculence was back, if not quite as pronounced as before. 'I knew you wouldn't make it this morning!'

'It seems neither of us did,' Lauren returned. 'Perhaps we could try again another morning? Not tomorrow, of course. You'll want to see your father off.' She paused. 'Are you coming back to the house?'

Kerry hesitated, glancing at Mick. 'Why?'

'I thought we might play tennis before lunch.'

'Have you trialled for the Olympics in that too?'

Lauren once more regretted having come out with that bit of information in an effort to impress the girl. 'No,' she said lightly. 'I just enjoy playing the game. It's up to you, of course.'

The refusal she'd been anticipating surprisingly failed to materialise. Kerry lifted her shoulders. 'OK. See you later,' she added to Mick.

'Has Mick been here long?' Lauren asked casually as the two of them made their way back through the trees.

'A couple of years,' Kerry confirmed. 'He's twenty.' She made it sound awesomely mature. 'He takes care of everything round the stables. He's the only one Dad trusts to ride Caliph. He's really wicked looking, isn't he?'

Taking the wicked as meaning terrific in teenage parlance, Lauren could imagine how the pony-tail, sharp-cut features and wiry build would appeal. Mick could be straight out of any one of half a dozen boy bands.

'Absolutely!' she agreed.

Kerry gave her a sharp sideways glance. 'Well, I wouldn't really expect *you* to think so!'

'Being far too old to appreciate modern youth, you mean?'

'You're more likely to fancy somebody like Dad.'

It was Lauren's turn to slant a glance. 'We're not starting on that tack again, are we? I know you suspect me of having ulterior motives in taking this job, but I really don't have any designs on your father.'

'You like him though, don't you?'

'Well…yes, I suppose so.' Lauren was beginning to flounder. 'I hardly know him.'

There was a speculative expression in her daughter's eyes. 'Dad said you'd come back to England to live, but John Batley says you only brought a couple of suitcases with you. That doesn't sound very much.'

'I brought everything that meant anything.' That much at least was the truth. 'I was taking a bit of a holiday before looking for a permanent job, but—'

'But you couldn't miss a chance like this.'

'No.' They were in sight of the house. Lauren briskened her tone. 'We might have time for a couple of games before lunch if we get our skates on.'

'I think it's too hot now for tennis,' Kerry decided. 'I'd rather go for a swim.'

'Fine by me.' Lauren would have agreed to any suggestion just to keep that rather more friendly note in her daughter's voice.

They went upstairs together, parting at Lauren's door. Of the three bathing suits she had brought with her, the plain black one-piece she used for speed swimming was the easiest to slip into. She donned the short cotton wrap she used as a dressing gown for cover, along with a pair of sandals.

Wearing a bright pink bikini, Kerry was already in the pool when she got there. So, Lauren was disconcerted to find, was Brad.

'I wondered where you'd got to,' he said.

Self-conscious in a way she'd never been before in her life, she slid off the wrap, seeing the blue eyes take on a deeper hue as they traversed every inch of her. She executed a clean dive, swimming underwater to surface on the far side.

The action had made her shoulder ache, so she stayed

where she was to rest it a moment or two. Brad surfaced suddenly in front of her, startling her because she hadn't seen him coming.

'That shoulder giving you trouble?' he asked.

'It's OK,' she assured him. 'I'd forgotten about it.'

Treading water, dark hair curling a little at the ends as it shed moisture, he surveyed her with that same deepened blue intensity. 'You,' he declared, 'are giving me one hell of a hard time!'

Lauren felt the surge in her pulse rate, the kick in her stomach muscles. It was an effort to keep her voice steady.

'I thought you took a cold shower?'

'I did,' he said. 'Not much good it did me when I saw you just now. That suit is scheduled to send blood pressure through the roof!'

'I didn't wear it to start any fires,' she defended.

'I'm not complaining. Well, yes, I suppose I am,' he admitted. 'I'm actually regretting having to leave to-morrow.'

'Hopefully, Kerry will be a great deal less opposed to me by the time you get back,' she said.

He accepted the change of subject with a glint, re-cognising the tactic for what it was. 'She can't fail to be. You've already made more headway than I'd ever have expected in so short a time. Where did you find her?'

'At the stables talking with Mick. I hear he rides Caliph.'

'He keeps all three exercised when necessary.' Brad paused. 'What do you think of him?'

Lauren hesitated, not quite sure of her ground. 'He's obviously very good with the horses.'

'He is. I meant on the whole.'

'I think Kerry might have a bit of a crush on him,' she admitted. 'But I'd doubt if there's anything to worry about from his side. He strikes me as having his feet far too firmly on the ground to risk jeopardising his job in any way.'

'I'd tend to agree, but you might keep an eye on him.'

'You can rely on me,' Lauren promised.

'I am,' he said.

Kerry swam over, the glance she winged from one to the other a mite suspicious. 'I thought we might have another race,' she said to Lauren.

'Best to leave it a few days until her shoulder's eased up,' Brad advised before Lauren could answer. 'I'll race you myself.'

She pulled a face. 'You always win!'

'There's always a first time,' he said. 'Two straight lengths?'

Lauren watched the pair of them head off to the end of the pool to start the competition, unable to keep the spark of jealousy fully at bay. Brad had the rest of his life to be with his daughter; she had so little time. Miss him though she certainly would the coming week, it would be good to have Kerry all to herself for a while.

He won the race, but only just—although she suspected him of holding back in the final few yards. Kerry was delighted. Next time, she declared, she'd definitely do it.

She retained her good mood all through lunch. Brad's casual suggestion that they spend the afternoon showing Lauren something of the area drew no protest. It proved an enjoyable afternoon. Lauren fell ever more in love with the rolling green and gold countryside, the beautiful old villages and historic monuments.

'It's another world!' she declared over a cream tea in

a tiny village near Warwick. 'We don't have anything remotely like this in Canada.'

'You have far more spectacular scenery,' Brad responded. 'And a hell of a lot more space. I'd have thought you might feel a bit hemmed in.'

'Not for a minute. I like the nearness of everything.' She laughed. 'That's a terrible way of putting it, but you know what I mean.' She looked across at Kerry, who was apparently engrossed in spreading jam on her scone prior to the cream. 'You're very lucky to live in such a lovely part of the world!'

'My school is in Cambridge,' came the unenthused answer. 'I'm there much more than I'm here.'

'Schooldays don't last forever,' said her father.

'You'll be telling me next that it's the best time of my life,' she rejoined, drawing a sudden grin.

'I wouldn't go as far as that. I hated mine.'

She looked at him in some surprise. 'You did?'

'A lot of the time. Who wants to be sitting in a schoolroom when there's a whole world out there to explore? Trouble is, without education it's a very hard place to be.'

'Have you thought about what you want to do when you do leave school?' Lauren asked lightly.

A spark of interest lit the pretty young face. 'I want to be a vet, specialising in horses.'

'That's a long, hard training,' Brad observed.

'I know,' she said. 'But not like school.'

'I think you'll make a great vet!' Lauren put in before Brad could pour the cold water she could almost hear coming on the latter statement. Kerry was right: there was a big difference between basic education and training for a career. Anyway, she might have something else entirely in mind at eighteen.

Five more years. Where would she be then? she wondered with a sudden dampening of spirits. Where would they all be?

Feeling Brad's eyes on her, she made haste to lift her mood. At least she had the coming few weeks.

They arrived back at Ravella at five-thirty to be greeted with the news that someone called Steven Dexter had phoned several times.

'He tried to reach you on your mobile number,' Mrs Perriman advised, 'but he couldn't get through. He said to contact him as soon as you came in.'

Brad went off immediately to make the call. With a couple of hours to go until dinner, Lauren suggested a session on the tennis court, but Kerry declined.

'I bet Dad has to go tonight to sort out whatever's gone wrong,' she said flatly.

'It might not come to that,' Lauren consoled, feeling more than a little depressed herself at the thought. 'If you don't want to play tennis, what *do* you feel like doing?'

'Like being on my own,' was the ungracious response. '*You* can do what you like!'

Lauren bit back the sharp retort that rose to her lips. Allowing herself to be drawn into retaliation was no solution. So things had seemed to be going well this afternoon. That didn't mean she'd cleared all the hurdles.

She hung around until Brad put in an appearance again, anticipating confirmation of Kerry's guess.

'Trouble?' she queried.

'Nothing that can't be handled,' he said. 'We'll sort it out on the plane.'

'You'll be leaving tonight, then?'

'No.' He regarded her speculatively. 'Were you hoping so?'

Lauren returned his gaze steadily. 'Kerry was upset that you might have to take an earlier flight.'

His mouth slanted. 'Then you can be the bearer of good news. I'll be leaving after breakfast as arranged. Anything you might need to know about while I'm away?'

She shook her head. 'Nothing I can think of. My job is simple enough.'

'A matter of opinion. Although the two of you seem to be getting along.'

'Up and down still, but it's early days yet.' She made a move. 'I'll go and tell her.'

Brad let her go without further comment. Taking it that Kerry would have gone to her room, she headed upstairs. Her knock on the bedroom door elicited an almost imperceptible response. Lauren took it as an invitation to come in.

She found her daughter seated at a desk holding a computer and peripherals. She was playing some kind of game from the looks of it. Taking her mind off the probability that Brad would be leaving tonight, Lauren assumed. Her appearance elicited little apparent interest, but at least she wasn't greeted with a scowl.

'Nice set-up,' she commented. 'I take it you're on the Internet?'

'Of course.' This time Kerry did look round. 'Are you computer literate too?'

The term made Lauren smile inwardly. 'I wouldn't call myself an expert, but I can get by. I came up to tell you your father isn't going to be leaving early after all.'

Kerry did her best to look as though the news was

of little count. 'I don't suppose it makes much difference. I bet *you're* glad though.'

'I think it's nice he doesn't have to rush off,' Lauren agreed readily. 'We could play Scrabble or something after dinner, maybe?'

'Dad doesn't play kids' games,' came the somewhat withering reply.

'Scrabble's a challenge for all ages,' Lauren countered. 'Do you have a set?'

Kerry indicated a tall, deep cupboard set against the nearby wall. 'It'll be in there, if it hasn't been thrown out by now.'

It was unlikely that anyone but she herself would have done any throwing out, Lauren reflected, going to take a look.

The conglomeration facing her when she opened the doors was daunting. It took her a full ten minutes to find what she sought, drawing out the familiar box with a triumphant, 'Eureka!'

'You won't get Dad to play,' Kerry reiterated.

'When did you last try him?'

The pause was brief. 'He doesn't have time.'

'He will have tonight.' Lauren was determined on that. 'I'll take the box with me and make sure nothing's missing, shall I?'

'If you like.' But it won't happen, was the unspoken rider.

Lauren winged a glance around the room with its plain cream walls and sleekly modern furnishings. Kerry's own choice, she assumed. The framed photograph on one of the bedside tables brought a sudden ache to her chest. Casually dressed, Brad had an arm about an auburn-haired young woman who could only be Claire, his free hand resting on the shoulder of the child in front of them. They were all three of them laughing.

'That was taken on my eighth birthday,' said Kerry, following her gaze. 'Mom was killed three months after.'

She sounded composed, but Lauren sensed the bleakness beneath. She felt much the same herself, if for rather different reasons. Claire had at least had eight years.

'She was very lovely,' she said.

Kerry made no answer, face closed. There was so much Lauren wanted to tell her, but no way she could do it without ruining her life altogether.

With no excuse to linger any further, she took her leave. There proved to be nothing at all missing from the Scrabble box. Lauren packed everything back in again, and set it aside to fetch downstairs later. Like it or not, Brad was going to join in a game, she vowed—though with little idea of how exactly she would get round an out-and-out refusal.

Surprisingly, considering Kerry's opinion, he raised no objection when she put the proposal after dinner.

'It's been a long time since I played word games though,' he said. 'I think a ten-point starter wouldn't be out of the way.'

'If anybody should have a starter, it should be me,' returned Kerry promptly. 'You've both had a lot longer to build up your vocabulary than I have.'

His laugh was spontaneous. 'OK, smarty pants, let's get to it!'

Eyes sparkling, she started setting the board out. Lauren gave Brad a warmly approving look, seeing his lips curve in amused response. They were gathered around a broad coffee-table, Brad and herself in chairs,

Kerry preferring to squat on the floor. Like any family spending an evening together, came the thought, bringing a sudden wave of longing. If only it could be true!

She dismissed the notion instantly. A pipedream—regardless of what Mrs P might think. The situation aside, Brad's interest in her was no more than he might have in any woman who attracted him. It could hardly be anything else.

Despite his claim, he finished up winning two games out of the four they played. He called a halt at half-past ten when Kerry could no longer smother her yawns.

'Time we were all turning in, anyway,' he said. 'Early start tomorrow.'

Kerry looked a little downcast again at the reminder, but she went off to bed without further protest. Lauren tidied the game away, while Brad poured nightcaps for them both.

'I actually enjoyed that,' he admitted, coming back across with the glasses. 'It's a good way of keeping the brain active.'

'I shouldn't have thought your brain was ever anything but,' she returned. 'Don't you get tired at times?'

'Of business matters, you mean?' A hint of a smile flickered across his lips. 'I do have other things in mind from time to time.' His brow creased as she put up a hand to rake back the hair that had fallen forward over her cheeks, throwing her profile into sharp relief. 'It's really odd, but I still keep feeling I've seen you before somewhere.'

'Maybe in a past life?' she quipped, anxious to steer him away from dangerous ground. 'I was a slave girl in old Istanbul last time round. Or so I'm reliably told.'

'And I was king of Siam!' Brad was laughing now.

'You don't really believe in all that regression business, do you?'

'I'm not sure,' she said. 'It could account for those moments of *déjà vu* most people have at times. I remember driving to Niagara a few years back, and suddenly getting a vivid mental picture of what lay around the next bend. I was spot on too—and I'd never been on that road before.'

'Hardly fits in with the Istanbul theme.'

'Oh, we're not stuck with just the one prior life. Or even with the same form in fact. I've always felt a definite affinity with lizards. Nothing to do all day but lie in the sun and catch a few flies. Sheer bliss!'

'You,' Brad declared, 'are sending me up!'

Lauren looked back at him in wide-eyed innocence. 'As if I'd dare!'

He grinned. 'I doubt if there's a man alive who could intimidate you. Not that intimidation is what most men would have in mind.'

This conversation was getting out of hand, warned a small voice at the back of her mind, but the urge growing in her overrode the caution. He wanted her, she knew. And she wanted him. Right now it was all she could think about.

'You're not most men,' she said softly, and saw the blue eyes spark.

He took the glass he'd given her, placing it along with his own on the coffee-table, then drawing her to her feet. The kiss brought the blood drumming into her ears and dropped the bottom right out of her stomach.

She couldn't have held back if she'd tried. Not from that. Her hands slid up behind his head, fingers twining into the thick dark hair as she answered the heady demand. He drew her closer against him, moulding her to

his shape with a possessiveness that thrilled her, rousing
her to an overwhelming need for more, for far, far more.

She shut out all dissenting voices when he turned her
towards the door.

CHAPTER SIX

HE TOOK her to his room, not hers. He didn't put on any lights, pulling her back into his arms to kiss her with a fervour that overrode every remaining vestige of sanity.

Stripped, he was magnificent: chest deep, stomach hard-packed with muscle, thighs taut. She allowed her senses full rein, pressing her lips into the damp whorls of wiry hair on his chest as she slid her hands slowly down his flanks to seek the vibrant essence of his manhood.

Brad said something guttural under his breath and swept her up to lay her on the bed. Starting at the hollow of her throat, he kissed his way down the full length of her body, his tongue caressing her tingling, peaking nipples like a flickering flame. Lauren clutched at the dark head when he lowered it to her parted thighs, almost unable to bear the exquisite sensation. 'Too much!' she heard her own voice pleading.

When he lifted himself away from her she thought for a heart-stopping moment that he was leaving her, but he was simply reaching into the bedside drawer. If she'd been capable of rational thought by then, the realisation of what he was doing might have brought her to her senses, but all she did feel was the mounting urgency.

She slid her hands over the broad shoulders when he lowered himself to her again, breath catching in her throat as they joined together. It felt so right to be with him like this. So utterly and completely right! Caught up in the age-old rhythm, she lost all sense of time and place, unaware of the sounds torn from her throat as she reached the ultimate peak.

She came back to reality by slow degrees, opening her eyes to find Brad propped on an elbow, smiling down at her.

'You drifted off,' he said. 'So did I. Hardly surprising considering the energy we expended between us.' He put up a hand to twist a tendril of damp hair from her face, sliding the back of his knuckles gently down her cheek. 'You're a revelation, do you know that? So cool and controlled on the surface, so wild underneath!'

Lauren damped lips gone dry, struggling to keep her newly warring emotions at bay. 'What time is it?'

'Just after midnight.' He dropped his hand lightly to her shoulder as she made a convulsive attempt to sit up. 'Relax. There's no hurry. We still have the whole night ahead of us.'

'You've an early start tomorrow,' she reminded him, trying to sound practical about it. 'You'll have need of a clear mind to deal with whatever it is you have to deal with.'

'It isn't my mind I'm concerned with right now.' He shifted his hand again, this time to her breast, bringing her to shuddering life with his mere touch. 'That's the way I feel too,' he said softly. 'I can't have enough of you, Lauren!'

Whatever *her* mind might be saying, body and soul weren't going along. She responded to him because she couldn't do anything else, returning his kisses in a kind of desperation.

It was just as tremendous this time. Lying drained in

his arms, his head on her breast, Lauren wished they could stay like this forever. It couldn't happen, of course. Eventually she was going to have to face the cold light of day. Making love with a man she'd met just a bare two days ago was nothing to be proud about in itself; doing it with the man her daughter called father was infinitely worse.

'I really must go,' she said thickly.

'I suppose so,' Brad agreed with reluctance. 'It would have been better the other way round, but—'

'But the protection was here,' she finished for him.

He lifted to look at her, brows drawn together. 'There was no slur intended, believe me!'

'It hadn't occurred to me to think there might be,' she said. 'It's a good habit to form.' She stirred restlessly, desperate now to be gone before she gave too much away. 'Let me up, please.'

He rolled away from her, lying on his back, gazing at the ceiling, while she scrambled to find her discarded clothing. She kept her mind as blank as possible. Dressed at last, she looked back at him hesitantly.

'I'll say goodnight, then.'

Sitting up now, expression impossible to read in the darkness, he stretched out a hand. 'I think I merit a little more than that. Come back here.'

Lauren went against her will, steeling herself against the impact of his kiss. It would have been all too easy to sink down into his arms again. She tore herself away with an effort, forcing a smile.

'You'd better get some sleep. You've a heavy day ahead of you.'

'What's the problem?' he asked softly. 'It's what we both wanted.'

'I know.' She searched her mind for some adequate

response. 'It's just not on, is it? It's only been two days!'

The firm mouth curved. 'If I'd had my way, it wouldn't even have been that long.' He paused, studying her face. 'You'd feel better about it if we'd known each other longer?'

'I'd feel better if it hadn't happened at all!' she claimed.

'You don't mean that,' he stated with masculine certainty. 'You were as carried away as I was!'

'That's not what I'm talking about. It isn't just the time element. I'm here to take care of your daughter.'

'Supposing I fired you? Would that make a difference?'

Her smile was faint. 'Not really.'

'Then stop talking rubbish!' He pulled her to him, his mouth unexpectedly tender. 'If it weren't for Kerry, we'd have missed knowing each other at all,' he murmured.

Lauren made a supreme effort to stay in control of the emotions he could so easily conjure in her. 'It's Kerry's needs I'm supposed to be fulfilling, not ours.'

'No reason why you can't do both.'

'And run the risk of her guessing what's going on?'

'Only if we're careless about it.' His tone firmed. 'Kerry means a lot to me, but I'm not cut out to play the role you seem to think I should be playing. I want you, and I'd say there's little doubt after tonight that you want me too.' He put a finger to her lips as she made to speak. 'I've said all I'm going to say for the moment. You know how I feel. Go and get some sleep.'

Lauren reached her own room without mishap, closing the door to stand for several minutes trying to sort herself out. Tonight had been wonderful, there was no denying that, but she should have had the strength of mind to hold out against what amounted to nothing more than lust!

Only it wasn't just that, was it? asked the treacherous little voice at the back of her mind. Brad aroused emotions far above and beyond the merely physical. She loved being with him, talking with him, seeing the blue eyes crinkle in amusement, his mouth slant in that slow, taunting smile. He was so right about the instant attraction. She'd felt it the moment he opened the door to her. What she hadn't allowed for was reciprocation on his part.

The problem now was just what he was going to expect from her on his return. To carry on a full-blown affair right under Kerry's nose was beyond her, if it wasn't beyond him. Men saw things so differently. Desire was to be indulged at any cost.

Whatever he might expect, she didn't have to go along with it, of course. He was hardly likely to toss her out on her ear for refusing to sleep with him again. After tonight's experience, it was going to be far from easy, but it had to be done.

Getting down to breakfast to find Brad already gone brought mingled relief and despondency. He'd left her a note to say there was a cash box in his desk from which she was to take any expenses over the coming few days, ending with just the bold scrawl of his name.

So what else did she expect? Lauren asked herself. Last night was last night. He'd probably had second thoughts about the whole affair himself by now.

Kerry was downcast too, the change in the weather no help. 'It's raining again!' she announced, gazing out of the window. 'So what now?'

'The horses still need exercising,' Lauren suggested. 'You'll have your own wet-weather gear, and I'm sure there'll be some I could use.'

Kerry considered her doubtfully. 'Dad said you should be resting your shoulder.'

'My shoulder's fine.' Lauren flexed it, surprised herself to feel no more than a twinge or two. The liniment had certainly done its job.

'You'll have to make do with the jacket Dad keeps in the tack room.' Kerry sounded a mite more upbeat. 'It will be a bit big, but it's all there is.'

'Great. Let's go and change, then.'

The rain had settled back to a fine drizzle by the time they reached the stables. There was no sign of Mick, although he'd obviously been there at some point, as the boxes had been mucked out.

'He'll have gone over to the gardener's shed for a cigarette,' Kerry guessed, looking a little despondent again. 'Dad put a ban on him smoking round the stables.'

'A good thing with all this straw around,' Lauren commented. 'No problem, anyway. We can do our own tacking up.'

It proved a bit painful hoisting the saddle, but not enough to put her off. Despite the less than clement weather, she enjoyed the ride. The knowledge that the overlarge jacket she was wearing over her sweater was Brad's was a stimulation in itself, reluctant though she was to acknowledge it. She had to put a tight rein on such responses if she was to finish up heart whole.

Kerry herself seemed to have got over her moodiness. With the ground wet, and slippy in parts, she made no attempt to put Diamond into a gallop, contenting herself with a brisk canter along the edge of a field before settling the mare down to a steady walk side by side with Lauren.

'You're not really all *that* bad for an amateur,' she said condescendingly. 'A bit more practice, and you'll be OK.'

Lauren fought to keep any element of irony from her voice. 'Thanks. I'm looking forward to doing this every day. You must really miss it in term time.'

'I have Diamond at school with me. There's stabling for twenty horses. Dad booked one for the rest of my time there.'

'Do you really dislike school as much as you made out yesterday?' Lauren ventured, and saw a reluctant smile touch her daughter's lips.

'It's not that bad, I suppose. I'd still rather be here going to day school though. There's a really good one the other side of Stratford. My best friend goes there.'

'Do I get to meet this friend some time?'

'Probably. She's away on holiday. In Italy.'

'You've never been abroad yourself?' Lauren asked, picking up on the wistful note.

'Not to Italy. I've been to France and Portugal and Greece, and Dad took me to Disneyworld in Florida at Easter, but I'd love to go to Venice and ride in a gondola!'

'You'll have to suggest it for next time.' Lauren winged a mental apology to the man she had at first believed so neglectful. The trip to Disneyworld almost certainly wouldn't have been his idea of a perfect vacation.

Leaving as early as he had, he was probably calling in at the office before going to the airport. As chairman of a large international company, he'd have a whole lot more than just this one contract to deal with. She vis-

ualised him striding into his office, flinging orders right,
left and centre—his secretary fussing over him with coffee and biscuits. A good-looking one almost definitely:
she couldn't imagine him settling for anything less.

She had to stop thinking about him, she told herself
forcefully. Nothing could come of it.

The rain had stopped and the sun was raising steam
from the damp earth when they returned to the stables.
Mick was back *in situ,* painting a door frame. Lauren
saw him discard something into the bin at his back as
they came in through the archway, but she didn't make
any comment.

It was apparent that Kerry would have preferred to
linger behind on her own, but Lauren played dense.

'I thought we might go into Stratford for lunch, then
maybe take that boat trip you were talking about,' she
said casually. 'If you still want to, that is?'

'I suppose,' was the somewhat ungracious reply.

Better than a kick in the teeth, at any rate, Lauren
thought drily, seeing Mick's sly smile. He was well
aware of Kerry's feelings, she reckoned. Which was
fine, providing he didn't try taking any advantage of
them.

Back at the house, she changed into trousers and
shirt, then went to pay a visit to the study. It was the
first time she'd been in here since the day of her arrival.
Despite Brad's instructions, she felt a sense of intrusion.

The desk had three drawers on each side. She found
the cash box in the top left, taking out what she thought
the day might cost from the considerable contents. She
would have been more than happy to pay for her daughter's entertainment herself, but he was hardly going to
allow that.

The day turned out better than she'd hoped. Apart

from a difference of opinion over the size of boat they should take out, and some discord with regard to the speed restrictions when Kerry took a turn at the wheel, things went surprisingly smoothly.

Kerry admitted on the way home that she'd actually enjoyed herself. 'If I had to have a supervisor at all, I suppose I could have done worse,' she said grudgingly.

'For small mercies may we be truly thankful,' Lauren murmured, drawing a sudden grin.

'I suppose I've been a bit of a pig to you, pushing you in the pool and all. Thanks for not telling Dad about that.'

'Whatever happens between you and me is between you and me,' Lauren returned. 'I fight my own battles.'

'Is that what I am to you—a battle?'

What she was to her, she couldn't afford to disclose, came the painful thought. Aloud, she said lightly, 'More of a skirmish, I'm hoping.'

The grin came again. 'I'll think about it.'

There was a definite improvement in atmosphere between them that evening. The earlier part, at least. Kerry's departure pleading tiredness at nine left Lauren contemplating an early night herself, when the phone rang around half-past nine. Brad wasted no time on preliminaries.

'I thought you'd probably be in bed if I left it till after we landed. How's it going so far?'

'All right.' Lauren was too surprised by the call to chat. 'Kerry's upstairs. I'll get her.'

'There isn't time. We'll be starting the descent any minute. Anyway, it's you I wanted to speak to.' He paused. 'About last night—'

'You don't need to worry,' she cut in swiftly, sensing

what was coming. 'It meant no more to me than it did to you.'

The line went dead before he could reply. Not that she had any doubt of what that reply would have been. With time to think about it, he would have realised just how impossible a situation it would have been if they'd continued the affair. The dejection she felt at the moment would pass. There were things far more important than lovemaking, no matter how good it had been.

She was lying through her teeth and she knew it. She'd already gone past the point of no return. What she had to do was live with it.

Although by no means a total transformation, Kerry's attitude continued to improve over the following days. They rode together each morning, used the pool whenever the weather was favourable, and played several games of tennis in addition to driving out to various places.

Lauren took advantage of a rainy afternoon when Kerry was showing signs of boredom to suggest she get out some family snapshots. She responded to Kerry's surprise that she could want to look at old photographs with a wholly spurious claim to have an interest in photography as an art.

The leather-backed album Kerry eventually fetched down from her room had been put together by a mother's hand, every stage of the child's development lovingly preserved on film. Her emotions under uncertain control, Lauren watched her daughter grow from heart-wrenching babyhood to laughing toddler, to proud five-year-old in her prep-school uniform and on to the gap-toothed eight-year-old portrayed in the family shot she had seen the other day. The snaps dwindled almost to nothing after that. Claire had so obviously been the one keenest on keeping record.

There were shots of mother and child together through the years too, and plenty with the three of them. The Brad of eight, ten, twelve years ago didn't look all that different: there was the same firmly moulded mouth and uncompromising jawline, the familiar smile, the vivid eyes. His hair was shorter and crisper these days, but it was still just as thick, with no hint of grey as yet in the darkness.

Kerry watched her curiously as she leafed slowly through the pages.

'They're not what you'd call works of art, are they?' she said.

'They're wonderful!' Lauren answered spontaneously, catching herself up a little too late. 'I mean, as a memento,' she hastened to add. 'So many people just take video film these days. It's nice to see a good old-fashioned album. Your mother—' she still found the word hard to say '—did a really good job keeping all this together.'

'She was good at everything.' There was pride in the statement. 'Dad told me you play the piano. I'll bet you're nowhere near as good as Mom was!'

Lauren refused to allow the disparagement to get to her. 'Probably not,' she agreed. She shut the album reluctantly, wishing she could hang on to it. 'I hear you play too.'

'Not for a long time.' The young face had closed up again. 'I'll take that upstairs.'

One step forward, two steps back, Lauren thought wryly as she went from the room.

Saturday saw the start of what was forecast to be another heatwave. The two of them were sunbathing by the pool when Brad put in a totally unexpected appearance around four. He was already changed into trunks and towelling robe.

'I got in half an hour ago,' he said. 'I took the red-eye last night, spent a couple of hours at the office this morning, then headed right home.'

Perching on the edge of Kerry's lounger, he eyed the two of them with quizzically lifted brows. 'So, what have *you* found to do with yourselves all week?'

'Tons!' Kerry answered. 'Lauren took me into Leamington for a whole new wardrobe. We went in every shop!'

'She needed a lot of things replacing.' Lauren took steps to eradicate the slightly defensive note in her voice. 'Styles are always changing.'

'No explanations necessary.' Brad sounded easy. 'What did you use for money? It sounds as if there might not have been enough in the cash box.'

'I have a couple of credit cards,' she said. 'I saved all the receipts.'

She reached for the sun cream she had already applied only moments before, avoiding his gaze. Keeping her feelings under cover was going to be one of the hardest things she'd ever been called on to do. She wished he'd stop looking at her; she could feel those eyes of his burning into her brain. Luckily, Kerry was busy examining a small reddened area on her thigh where some insect appeared to have bitten her.

'I'm going in,' he said, getting up again. 'A swim might drive out the cobwebs.'

He dropped the robe on the end of the lounger, and took the few steps to the pool edge to execute a clean dive. Lauren watched him power end to end of the pool, water-beaded shoulders glinting in the sun. She ached to join him, to feel his lips on hers, his body hard against her.

He came out after completing more than twenty lengths, towelled himself roughly down, then drew up another lounger next to hers.

'Lizards definitely have the right idea,' he murmured, stretching out.

'How long are you going to be home for?' asked Kerry, sounding as if she'd already prejudged the answer.

'I'm OK till the board meeting Monday afternoon.' He added lightly, 'How would you fancy a couple of days in town yourself?'

She sat up, eyes lit. 'Seriously?'

'It's not something I'd joke about. Lauren too, of course. I'm certainly not leaving you to run around London on your own. The two of you can do your own thing during the day, and we'll join forces for the evening. Maybe take in a couple of shows. It's been a while since I went to the theatre myself.'

Anticipating some discord on Kerry's part at the idea of having her along, Lauren was surprised by the ready response.

'Great! We can do some more shopping!'

Brad gave a mock-groan. 'Mad fool that I am!' He turned his head to view Lauren's face, making her thankful for the semi-protection offered by her sunglasses. 'I take it you'll have no objection to coming along?'

Considering that an objection from her would result in Kerry losing out too, there was only one answer she could make. 'None at all. Nice idea. Where will we stay?'

'My flat only has two bedrooms, so it will have to be a hotel.'

'We can share,' offered Kerry magnanimously. 'I don't mind.'

Warmed beyond measure, Lauren directed a smile at the girl. 'Fine by me.'

'That's settled, then. We'll drive up Monday morning.' Brad settled back again, clasping his hands behind his head and closing his eyes. 'For now, we'll make the most of this.'

Lauren did her best to relax again herself, but found it impossible. With barely six inches of space between her lounger and his, he was far too close. She could see the firmly muscled thighs on the periphery of her vision, the tautly stretched black trunks outlining the part of him that had been a part of her not so very long ago. The heat spreading through her had nothing to do with the sun. She wanted him so badly she could scarcely contain it.

Torn between conflicting emotions when Kerry got up and dived into the pool, she was on the verge of following her example when Brad said levelly, 'We need to talk.'

'About what?' she prevaricated.

'You know about what.' He lifted up, propping himself on a bent elbow to cast a lingering glance down her shapely length. 'I think you misunderstood what I was trying to say when I phoned. There was no question of my not taking what happened between us seriously. I'd thought about little else all day.' His tone roughened. 'I'm having the devil of a job keeping my hands to myself right now. You have the most wonderful body!'

'Thanks.' The word was dragged from her.

'You'd rather be admired for your mind?'

'I like it to be recognised that I have one,' she retorted shortly.

'Did I give the impression that I doubted it?' The smile was in his voice as well as his eyes. 'You suit me in every sense. I'm hoping I do the same for you.'

Unfortunately only too much, she could have told him. She stiffened as he reached out for her sunglasses, unprepared to face the blue gaze naked, as it were. 'Don't!' she jerked out. 'Kerry…'

'She isn't looking,' he said, but he let the glasses stay, lying back again with a sigh. 'I agree this is neither the time nor place. It can wait till later.'

So she'd been wrong about his loss of interest, Lauren reflected. Not that it made any difference. She didn't dare allow herself any further involvement.

With the master of the house *in situ* again, dinner was restored to its usual seven-thirty timing. Brad's suggestion that they take a walk in the grounds after the meal received little interest from Kerry. She had better things to do, she said. Lauren agreed with some reticence, wondering how best to put what she had to say.

It proved more difficult even than she had anticipated. What she wanted to do and what she *had* to do were two very different things, she acknowledged ruefully. Brad was everything she could have looked for in a man—everything any woman could look for. While she doubted she'd be fired for refusing him any further intimacies, he was hardly going to accept it lightly. What she wasn't sure of was her ability to hold out against any persuasions he might bring to bear.

He made no immediate attempt to approach the subject, strolling at her side, hands thrust casually into trouser pockets.

'You and Kerry seem to have made real progress since I left,' he observed.

'Yes, I think we have,' Lauren agreed, only too ready to put off the moment of truth. 'We like a lot of the same things. That's been a big help.' She paused, casting a swift sideways glance at the strong profile. 'You haven't said how your business trip went.'

He shrugged. 'Well enough, after a few false starts. I'd hoped to be back earlier than this.' He came to a halt as they emerged from the trees into a wide glade, indicating a seat positioned to take advantage of the view. 'Why don't we sit here for a few minutes?'

Lauren made no demur. Sitting or walking, the moment had to come.

'I think we'd better have things clear between us,' she said without preamble. 'What happened the other night was a mistake. One I've no intention of repeating. If you need a woman in your bed, you'll just have to look elsewhere. I'm—'

The words were cut off as Brad pulled her to him, his mouth claiming hers with an ardour that set her on fire. A part of her tried to resist, but it was a hopeless struggle against overwhelming odds.

'You're worth more than that,' he said roughly when he finally lifted his head. 'A whole lot more!' He cupped her face between his hands, eyes filled with an emotion that rocked her to the core. 'I haven't felt like this about any woman since Claire. I thought I'd never feel this way again. I want you to marry me, Lauren.'

CHAPTER SEVEN

THIS couldn't be happening! Lauren thought dazedly. She had to be hallucinating!

Except that the man holding her felt only too real—looked only too real.

'You can't be serious,' she got out.

'Never more so,' he said. 'I've had all week to think about it. Kerry was the only problem, but the two of you seem to be getting along so well.' He kissed her again, the tenderness more telling than any passion. 'I love you,' he murmured against her lips.

'You can't,' she whispered. 'It isn't possible!'

'To fall in love in a few days?' He smiled, shaking his head. 'A fortnight ago I'd have said the same thing. That was before I knew you. I'm not normally given to impulsive action, but, having found you, I'm not letting go. You might not feel quite the same way about me as yet, but you're going to.'

'I am?' she said dazedly.

'You can bet on it. We've everything going for us. A lot more than most, in fact.'

'You don't know...anything about me.' The words were dragged from her.

'I know all I need to know. You're beautiful, intelligent, sexy, humorous—what more could a man ask for?'

Honesty, she thought painfully. If he knew the truth, none of this would be happening.

The confession trembled on her lips, but a stronger

force held it back. If she took that step she stood to lose everything. She loved this man, and he loved her. Did anything else really have to matter?

Brad searched her face, sensing the struggle going on inside her. 'What are you thinking?'

The words formed themselves. 'I think I must be dreaming.'

'Does that mean what I think it means?'

She drew a shaky breath, abandoning the last tattered remnants of principle. 'That I'm in love with you? You can bet on it!'

He laughed. 'Then I take it the answer's yes?'

Lauren put her lips back to his in a sudden rush of emotion, stirring him to immediate and passionate response. Still warm from the sun, the grass was a welcoming mattress, the coolness of his hands on her heated skin a stimulant in themselves. Not that stimulation was necessary. She needed this as much as he did. Perhaps even more. She didn't want to think, only to feel.

He stayed with her after the tumultuous climax, bearing his weight on his elbows as he watched her emerge from oblivion.

'A perfect match,' he stated softly. 'You hold nothing back.'

Nothing but the most important thing of all, came the thought, thrust aside before it could make too much impact.

'You don't make it possible to hold back.' She put up her hands to cup his face, much as he had done with her earlier, smoothing her fingers over the hard male cheekbones. 'You're a man of many parts, Bradley Laxton. And all of them sensational!'

'Keep thinking like that,' he said. 'But don't stop there. I want more from this marriage than sex alone.'

'You'll be getting it,' she promised. 'I've missed you so much this last week!' She gave a shaky smile. 'I never imagined for a moment that you could feel like this about me. I thought you were just...'

'After a temporary bedmate?' he finished for her as she let the words trail. 'I might have had just that in mind right at first, but you had me well and truly hooked within hours.'

Lauren kept her tone as light as possible. 'Maybe that was my aim. You have to admit, you're quite a catch!'

'Some might see things that way, but I'd doubt you have an avaricious bone in your body,' he rejoined.

'Oh, I don't know about that!' she said smiling.

The blue eyes crinkled at the corners. 'Watch it, lady. I'll not stand for mockery!' He kissed the end of her nose before lifting himself reluctantly upright. 'We'd better get back before Kerry takes it into her head to come looking for us.'

Lauren sat up unsteadily to adjust her own clothing, spirits taking a plunge. There was no way Kerry was going to accept it. She'd conclude what she'd suspected from the first: that her so-called carer had inveigled her way into the house with the object of finding a rich husband.

'It's far too soon to spring something like this on her,' she said hesitantly.

'So, we'll wait a while. I can go along with that. Just.' On his feet now, Brad extended a hand to help her to hers, holding her there in front of him for a moment to scan her face with that same intensity of emotion. 'I can go along with anything other than losing you.'

'Me too,' Lauren said softly. 'I've never felt this way about anyone before.'

'But you're still worried about Kerry's reaction. She'll come round. There's a huge difference in her attitude towards you already.'

'There's a huge difference between accepting something she knows is only for a limited period and this,' Lauren countered. 'She hates the thought of you marrying anyone at all.'

His jaw firmed. 'I'm afraid she'll just have to get used to the idea.'

The only alternative was for her to walk out on the whole situation, Lauren thought, knowing she was incapable of that kind of sacrifice. It would be up to her to win Kerry over—to get her to see the advantages to be had. It would take time, but that would no longer be at a premium. There was even a chance that arrangements could be made for her to leave boarding-school and start the new term alongside this friend of hers. It might help her see things in a better light.

It was almost dark, the stars already glinting in a sky clear of even the smallest cloud. Brad put a proprietorial arm about her shoulders as they started back to the house.

'I never asked you about your family,' he said. 'Are your parents still in Canada?'

Up until this moment, Lauren hadn't given them a thought herself. Their reaction to the news wasn't hard to imagine. So far as they were concerned, she was a long-lost cause.

'They are,' she said. 'Living in Vancouver now.' She hesitated, not sure how best to say it. 'I don't see all that much of them. We fell out when I refused to apply for naturalisation along with them. Obviously I'll be telling them about you, but they might not be all that enthusiastic.'

'Sounds as though we're in pretty much the same boat,' Brad observed. 'So it's just us. That's fine by me.'

It wasn't just the two of them though, was it? Lauren thought heavily. There was the secret she carried. She owed him the truth, she knew, but she couldn't bring herself to do it for fear he might take the same view Kerry was almost certainly going to take, and believe she'd set out to ensnare him. To lose him now would be more than she could bear—to say nothing of losing all future contact with her daughter too.

Kerry was still out when they got in. Brad poured them both a drink, eyeing her speculatively as he handed her the glass.

'Still worrying about Kerry's reaction?'

'I'm still in shock over the whole thing,' Lauren prevaricated. She searched the lean features. 'Are you really sure this is what you want, Brad?'

'I don't make a habit of asking women to marry me.' He studied her upturned face, mouth curving. 'You don't realise your own power. You came, I saw, I was conquered! There's certainly no doubt on my side. I don't want there to be any on yours.'

Short of blurting out the real reason for her hesitation, there was only one answer she could give. 'There isn't.'

'Then that's all that matters.' He took a seat beside her on the sofa, following the curve of her hair with a finger to lightly trace the shape of her lips. 'We're going to be good together. Not just in bed—though that's certainly not a minor factor—but in everyday life too. I need someone I can talk with, laugh with, play the fool with occasionally. Someone I can rant to when things don't go quite to plan, argue the toss with over differences of opinion. Does that come anywhere near to your idea of a happy marriage?'

'Close enough.' She hesitated before saying softly, 'Is that the kind of relationship you and Claire had?'

The blue eyes remained steady. 'In many ways. But no two loves are ever exactly the same. Claire had a very blithe personality. The only time I ever saw her really down was when she found she was unable to have children herself. Even then, she didn't stay down long. She was making enquiries about adoption within the week. Six months later, we had Kerry.'

Lauren yearned to hear more about those early days in her daughter's life, but she shrank from stirring up too many memories.

'Does it matter to you that I've been married before?' Brad asked, watching the play of expression across her face.

She shook her head, able to make that denial in all honesty. 'Not in the least. I just hope I can live up to her.'

'There's no doubt of it,' he declared. 'Not in my mind.'

About to draw her to him, he pulled himself up abruptly as the door was pushed open. Kerry paused on the threshold, the gaze she rested on the two of them sharpened.

'Are you discussing me?' she demanded.

It was Lauren who answered, only too relieved by the misconstruction. 'We were talking about London, and what the two of us might do while your father's otherwise engaged.'

Hazel eyes fired indignantly. 'What about *my* ideas?'

'I'm quite sure they'll be taken into account,' said

Brad drily. 'What have you been up to anyway? I thought you'd gone to bed.'

'I've been reading,' she said. 'I was going to the kitchen to get a drink when I heard you talking. Have you forgotten it's the village gala tomorrow?'

'I had,' Brad admitted. 'What about it?'

'We should all go,' she said.

'It sounds a great way to spend the day,' Lauren enthused. 'I haven't been to a gala in years!'

Brad put up his hands. 'All right, all right, you talked me into it, the pair of you! Not the whole day though. That would be asking just a little *too* much.'

Kerry pulled a face at him. 'Sacrifices have to be made by everyone. It opens at ten.'

She disappeared before he could answer, leaving him torn between amusement and exasperation. 'Give an inch, lose a mile!' he observed.

'Give an inch, gain several yards,' Lauren corrected. 'She said *all*. That included me. This time last week she'd have turned her nose up at the very notion.'

'This time last week, she hardly knew you,' he said. 'It's amazing how far you've got in a few days. By the time we tell her the news, the two of you should be on a good enough footing to make it more easily acceptable.'

Lauren hoped he was right. That would be one concern less, at least. The rest she would just have to deal with as and when. How was another matter.

Brad drew her to him, feathering her lips open to explore the soft inner flesh with the very tip of his tongue in a manner that sent tremors through her whole body. She answered instinctively, wantonly, fingers seeking between the buttons of his shirt for contact with warm skin and wiry body hair, mind filled with nothing but the emotions of the moment.

She came down to earth again with a thud when he suggested they should go to bed, fighting her own instincts.

'We can't,' she said. 'It's too risky. Supposing Kerry catches on?'

Brad drew back enough to view her face, his expression discordant. 'What are you saying? That we steer clear of any intimacy at all until after we're married?'

'No. Well, not exactly. I mean…' She broke off, lifting her shoulders in a helpless gesture. 'It isn't going to help anything if Kerry suspects we're sleeping together. She's not unaware of what we adults can get up to.'

The weak joke failed to raise even a glimmer of a smile. 'So, we'll just have to be careful. Starting now. I want you with me, Lauren. Tonight, and every night possible.'

He got to his feet, extending a hand, his jaw firmly set. 'Coming?'

If she refused, she'd not only be going against her own needs, but also putting the mere possibility of Kerry finding out about them before his, she conceded, taking the hand. As he'd said, they would just have to be careful.

Secure in the knowledge of his feelings for her, she found their lovemaking even more ecstatic. He was such a superb, unselfish lover, intent on giving her the utmost pleasure before allowing himself relief—introducing her to erogenous zones she hadn't even know existed until now.

She relinquished all inhibition herself, thrilling to the responses she could draw from him. They were so perfectly tuned to each other, sensitive to every nuance. What he made her feel was so much more than just sexual satisfaction, Lauren acknowledged in the hazy, lazy aftermath. Love was the only word that fitted.

The gala was already well under way when they got to the ground at eleven. Kerry darted off immediately on her own pursuits, leaving the two of them to wander around the various stalls. Brad was greeted from all sides.

The extremely attractive, dark-haired woman they bumped into by the coconut shy proved an exception, the look she gave him frosty enough to freeze milk.

'Let's move on,' she said to her male companion.

'Friend of yours?' Lauren queried blandly.

Brad lifted his shoulders. 'She's the one I was seeing last Saturday night. First and last date. I hadn't met you when I made it.'

'Apparently, she expected rather more from you than she got.'

'Apparently.' He sounded singularly undisturbed. 'All in the past. It's the future I'm looking to now.'

Lauren glanced his way, heart jerking as she met the vivid gaze. It was still hard to believe he felt the way he did about her. Feelings that would die a swift death if he ever discovered the truth about her, for sure, yet just how long could she hope to keep her secret?

'You're looking pensive again,' he observed. 'Still worrying about Kerry's reaction?'

'It's bound to be a shock for her,' she said. 'Especially considering the time element.'

'She'll get over it.'

Lauren hesitated before making the suggestion. 'There are ways of making things easier for her to accept. She'd love to swap boarding-school for the one her friend goes to near Stratford. It could even be possible to arrange it for the start of the autumn term.'

Brad regarded her thoughtfully, oblivious to the crowds milling about them. 'You're prepared to be a stay-at-home wife?'

'Staying at home doesn't mean vegetating. There are a thousand things I could find to do. I could start a crèche, for instance.'

'Like hell you could!' He was smiling, recognising the gambit for what it was. 'You'll have enough on handling the one.'

'You agree, then?' she asked. 'You'd let her transfer?'

'It would depend on whether Brookfields has a place available.' He sounded a little restrained. 'You certainly have her interests at heart.'

'Yours too,' she said, aiming to inject a little humour. 'Think how much easier life would be with a totally *happy* teenager about the place!'

'You reckon a change of school is all it's going to take?'

'It will certainly help.' She put a hand on his arm in instinctive appeal. 'I want this to work, Brad. For all of us!'

'It will,' he assured her.

Kerry appeared through the crowds, accompanied by a boy around her own age whose shock of bright ginger hair stood out like a beacon.

'Adrian's at Brookfields,' she announced without preamble. 'He knows Sarah.'

'We're in the same form,' he confirmed. 'Is it OK if Kerry comes to my birthday party tonight?'

'Where?' Brad asked.

'It's just up the road. Oaks Farm?'

'You're Neil Harris's son?'

'Yes. You know my dad?'

'We've met a few times.'

Fairly dancing with impatience, Kerry burst out, 'Can I go, then?'

'I don't see any reason why not.' Brad looked back to the boy. 'I'll drop her off. What time?'

'Half-past six. Dad's doing a barbecue. You and Mrs Laxton can come too, if you like. There'll be plenty of other adults there.' The last on a faintly resigned note.

'Thanks, but I think we'll pass,' Brad answered before Kerry could cut in with the correction ready on her lips. 'Half-past six it is.'

'Great! Bet I can beat you on the roll-a-penny!' he challenged Kerry.

'Not a hope!' she responded at once, forgetting what she'd been about to say.

Lauren let out a breath as the two of them took off again. 'That,' she said, 'was a real sticky moment!'

'I don't see why,' Brad returned equably. 'It might even have planted the idea in her head.'

Doubting it, she lightened her voice to say jestingly, 'I've only just realised—I'll be Lauren Laxton. It sounds like a character from *Superman!*'

He laughed. 'Call it fate. Lois Lane was my ultimate fantasy when I was a boy.'

It was a fantasy she was living right now, Lauren reflected. Her fear was waking up from it.

The gala was well organised, with entertainment for all ages. Brad won a coconut and a goldfish, handing both back to be competed for again. They ate freshly cooked hamburgers for lunch, washed down with bottled shandy from the refreshment tent, then watched a display by the police-dog handlers.

By two o'clock, he'd had enough. They went looking for Kerry, finding her with a small group of friends over by the swing boats. She made it plain that she wasn't yet ready to leave, but Brad gave her no option. Lauren couldn't blame him for refusing to leave her to make her own way home—although she would probably have given in to the plea for a bit more time herself.

The atmosphere in the car was heavy, to say the least. All Lauren's attempts to lighten her daughter's mood met with failure. Brad's patience ran out before they even reached the house.

'Carry on like this, and you can forget about tonight,' he threatened.

'I don't want to go now, anyway!' Kerry declared sulkily. 'They'll all be laughing at me, being dragged off like that!'

'If they are, they're not the kind of friends you need.'

There was no answer from the rear. Lauren bit down on her own tongue, metaphorically speaking. She wasn't so far past her own girlhood that she couldn't remember how it felt to be shown up in front of one's friends. Especially new friends.

Kerry got out of the car without a word the moment it came to a standstill, stalking off indoors without a backward glance.

'There are times,' Brad said shortly, 'when I wonder why I bother!'

'You've been through puberty yourself,' Lauren defended. 'You must remember what it's like to be treated like a kid when you don't feel like one any more.'

'You'd let her run riot if she was yours, then?'

It took Lauren everything she had to keep her expression unrevealing, her voice calm. 'No, of course not. I'm not saying you were wrong to insist she came home with us, just that it wouldn't have hurt to stay a little longer ourselves. How often does she get the chance to mingle with the local youth?'

'Certainly not as much as she would if she attended Brookfields.' He paused, an odd expression in his eyes. 'Just which of us is most important to you?'

'That's not fair!' she protested. 'It's a totally different thing.'

'Is it?'

'Yes!' She was desperate to convince him, knowing it unlikely yet terrified he might take a stab in the dark. 'What I feel for you bears no comparison. How could it possibly?'

He looked suddenly wry. 'I never thought it possible to feel jealous of my own daughter.'

'I love you,' she said, desperate to convince him. 'You're a man in a million, Brad!'

The blue eyes kindled. 'I'll settle for the first bit.'

Lauren met his lips halfway, putting heart and soul into the kiss. Hands buried in the golden fall of her hair, he held her close, his mouth possessive.

'Let's go on in,' he murmured.

'It's barely three o'clock,' she protested half-heartedly.

'I know.' The devilish sparkle was back in his eyes. 'More than four hours till dinner. It might just be long enough.'

With Kerry sulking in her room, the cleaners long finished for the day, and Mrs P probably whiling away the afternoon in her own apartment, there was no one to see the pair of them heading upstairs. Lauren lost sight of everything else in his arms. Making love with

Brad was an experience she couldn't have enough of. His knowledge of just where and how to touch to have her writhing in ecstasy might indicate how many women he must have known in the past to have acquired that degree of expertise, but past was the operative word.

It was gone six when they finally called time. Lauren reached her room without running into anyone, and spent half an hour packing a bag for tomorrow's trip before changing for dinner.

The pleasurable ache in the lower half of her body was a constant reminder of the afternoon's excesses. She couldn't regret a minute of it, but neither could she keep from thinking about the way she'd abandoned Kerry at a time when she'd needed someone. Even if her overtures had been refused, it would have shown concern.

It was a surprise, but a happy one, to hear from Mrs Perriman when she went down that Brad was running Kerry to the party at Oats Farm.

The housekeeper made no comment, but the twinkle in her eyes spoke volumes.

Kerry had pulled out all the stops, Brad said on his return. 'I was always a soft touch when it comes to tears,' he admitted. 'And she knows it, the little demon! We're going out to dinner ourselves, by the way.'

'So Mrs P tells me.' Lauren hesitated. 'I think she might suspect something.'

He looked unconcerned. 'Does it matter?'

'Well, no, providing she doesn't say anything to Kerry.' She caught herself up, sensing his attitude harden a fraction. It had to happen some time; she could almost hear him saying it. Only not just yet. Not until her relationship with her daughter was on a firmer footing. 'Where are we going for dinner, anyway?'

'A little place I know near Stratford,' he said. 'The table's booked for eight o'clock, so we'd better get off. I told the Harrises we'd pick Kerry up no later than ten-thirty. They'll probably have had enough themselves by then, judging from the throng down there. I think they must have invited everybody in a twenty-mile radius!'

'Maybe we should have gone ourselves after all,' Lauren ventured.

'That would *really* have pleased a certain person,' came the dry reply. 'There'll be time enough for getting together with the neighbours, if that's what you fancy doing.'

She didn't. Not yet at any rate. She had quite enough to be going on with.

Converted from three cottages knocked into one, the restaurant was exclusive both in decor and clientele. The food was superlative, every dish a gourmet's delight. Lauren finished off with a lemon mousse to die for.

'That,' she declared, 'was pure heaven!'

Brad studied her in the candle glow, gaze travelling from the emerald brightness of her eyes down the smooth curve of her cheek to the soft fullness of her mouth. 'A classy setting for a classy woman,' he said. 'I'm not sure just how long I can wait to make certain of you.'

If it was just the two of them, she wouldn't want to wait either, Lauren admitted. Not the way she felt about him.

'You *are* certain of me,' she assured him. 'I'm not going anywhere.' She felt her insides turn fluid at the look in the blue eyes, still hardly able to believe herself

capable of rousing that depth of emotion in a man.
'You're making me blush,' she claimed.

He reached across and took her hand where it rested
on the damask cloth, raising it to his lips. 'Irresistibly!'

If only there were no secrets between them, she
thought achingly. Why didn't she confess the truth and
have done with it?

She knew why, of course. Because there was a very
real chance that he would suspect her of playing him
along with this very situation in mind. Not just for
Kerry's sake, but for her own too, she had to carry it
through. Perhaps there might come a time when she
could come clean, but it certainly wasn't yet.

It was almost a quarter to eleven when they got to
the farm. The party was to all intents and purposes over,
although a few adult stragglers still remained. A pleasant couple in their late thirties, the Harrises brushed
Brad's apology for their tardiness in picking Kerry up
aside. She was, they said, welcome to come over any
time.

Kerry had little to say on the way home. Lauren put
her silence down to tiredness. A theory borne out when
her offer to help pack, on discovering that no prepara-
tions had been made for the coming trip, was accepted
without demur.

'You *did* enjoy the party?' she asked when the two
of them were alone in the bedroom sorting out what to
take.

The young face lit up briefly. 'Of course I did. It was
great!'

'But?' Lauren prompted.

'But what?'

'You're not a hundred per cent happy about things,
are you?'

For a moment or two it seemed she wasn't going to get an answer, then Kerry let out a sudden sigh.

'I wish I didn't have to go away to school any more.'

Lauren forced back the words that rose instinctively to her tongue. Reassurance on that score would call for explanations as to why and how, with the reaction hardly likely to be favourable at this juncture, regardless of the advantages. Another couple of weeks could make all the difference if she played things the right way.

'It's a difficult situation,' she said carefully. 'The solution might be if your father got married again.'

Alarm leapt in the girl's eyes. 'You think he might be considering marrying this Diane woman?'

Lauren shook her head, able to reassure her on that point at least. 'Not a chance. There was nothing between them.'

Kerry gazed at her dubiously. 'How do you know?'

'He told me.'

'Why would he tell *you?*'

Lauren floundered for a moment. 'It…just came out in conversation,' she said weakly. She indicated a pile of clothing taken from a drawer. 'Which of these tops do you want to take?'

Sidetracked, Kerry came to look, discarding only three of the eight or nine lying there. 'You never know,' she said in response to Lauren's raised eyebrows.

She seemed rather more upbeat by the time they parted for the night. The hall was in darkness when Lauren took a look over the gallery rail. Likewise the other wing. With the time coming up to midnight, and an early start scheduled for the morning, it was hardly surprising if Brad had decided to spend the night alone, she supposed, although she had to admit to a certain chagrin that he could even contemplate it.

She returned quietly along the corridor to her own room, stifling an exclamation on finding him waiting for her in the bed. Obviously nude beneath the sheet drawn across at waist level, shoulders bronzed in the lamplight, he lit a fire inside her. There was little chance of Kerry popping in on them, but she turned the key in the lock anyway before going to join him, secure in their privacy.

CHAPTER EIGHT

THEY reached the capital just before midday after an uneventful drive. The flat was part of a warehouse conversion overlooking the river. Ultra-modern in design, it was totally different from Lauren's expectations.

'Convenience,' said Brad, noting her surprise. 'I'm due in the meeting at half-past two,' he added. 'If we're going to have lunch, we'd better make tracks now. You can unpack later.'

The car was left in the basement garage. Finding anywhere to park at this hour would be virtually impossible. They took a taxi to City Rhodes, passing the time of day with the famous young chef himself, who was paying a fleeting publicity visit. Kerry took it all in her stride, leading Lauren to the conclusion that this was by no means the first time she'd sampled the city high life.

'I've fetched her out of school the occasional weekend,' Brad confirmed when she put the question while Kerry was away from the table for a few minutes. 'At least there's no shortage of entertainment here.'

'She told me you took her to Disneyland at Easter,' Lauren said. 'That can't have been much fun for you.'

'Actually, I thoroughly enjoyed it.' He grinned at the look on her face. 'Mention second childhood, and you'll do penance!'

'As if such a thought would cross my mind!' She scrutinised the strongly carved features, the decorous grey suit and pristine white shirt, trying to imagine him zooming around on the glorified fairground rides. 'Are you really serious?'

'Really,' he said. 'There's a lot more to it than you'd think. You'll need to see it for yourself to know what I'm talking about. I dare say Kerry wouldn't turn her nose up at another trip.'

Lauren was sure of it. What she couldn't get her head round was the future he was mapping out. Little more than a week ago he hadn't even been aware of her existence.

'Still doubting me?' he asked.

'Not you yourself, just all this,' she admitted. 'You live in a world I could never have aspired to. It's going to take some getting used to.'

'What is?' asked Kerry, sliding back into her seat.

'Being back on home ground,' Lauren answered swiftly. 'Or virtually. I was born in Harrow.'

'Why did you go to Canada?' asked the girl curiously.

'My father was transferred there by his firm.'

'Did *you* want to go?'

Lauren's smile felt a little stiff. 'I didn't have much choice.'

'Do you have any brothers and sisters?' Kerry pursued.

'Afraid not.' Lauren could feel Brad's gaze on her, sure he must recognise her discomfiture. She was relieved to see the waiter approaching with dessert menus.

By the time she'd chosen what she wanted, Kerry had forgotten what they'd been talking about. Brad made no attempt to return to the subject either, though she could sense a certain speculation in his regard. She'd brought the subject up to get out of one hole, only to land herself in another. He suspected she was hiding something.

They parted company outside the restaurant, having arranged to meet back at the flat at half-past five. Given a free choice, Kerry opted for a visit to Harrods to start with, going on from there to Harvey Nichols. Lauren tried on a few items herself at her urging, finishing up with a caramel silk suit costing more than she'd ever spent on a single outfit in her life before.

'You can wear that at dinner tonight,' Kerry declared at the cash desk. 'Dad's sure to take us somewhere special!'

'This will take you anywhere, madam,' stated the sales assistant, securing the distinctive carrier. 'An excellent choice with your colouring. The shade would be good on your daughter too,' she added.

Lauren felt her face go first hot and then cold. Luckily, Kerry had moved away to look at a display. Not that the remark would have been likely to give her any food for thought if she'd heard it, Lauren assured herself.

It was almost half-past six when they reached the flat, to find Brad already changed for the evening.

'We got caught up in the rush hour,' Lauren explained. 'It took ages to get a taxi.'

'It might have been an idea to keep an eye on the time,' he said shortly. 'You'd better hurry up and get ready. I've theatre tickets booked. We'll have to eat later.'

'Bet he thought we'd been mugged or something,' remarked Kerry in the room they were sharing. 'Are you going to wear the suit you bought?'

Lauren shook her head. 'There isn't going to be time for any major titivating.' She opened the suitcase still waiting to be unpacked, extracting a cream jersey tunic that needed no ironing. 'This will do me.'

Kerry chose a dress herself, flashing a grin. 'Better not irk Dad any more by turning up in trousers. I'll use his bathroom. See you in fifteen.'

Lauren spent several minutes taking her hair up in a smooth sweep, hoping the pins would hold throughout the evening. The high-heeled sandals increased her five-feet-seven by a good three inches, which still left her short of another three at least to match Brad's height. A big man in every sense of the word, she thought.

She returned to the spacious living area to find him laying down the law regarding the eyeliner and mascara Kerry had applied with a somewhat over-enthusiastic hand.

'You're such a fuddy-duddy!' she stormed, before taking herself back to the bathroom to remove the stuff. 'We're going to be even later now!'

'Not my doing,' Lauren disclaimed as the blue gaze turned her way.

'So where *did* she get it?' he demanded.

'I wouldn't know. She certainly didn't buy it this afternoon. I agree about the eyes, though I don't think a touch of lipstick would look amiss,' she added mildly. 'It's a generally accepted thing these days.'

'Not by me. Not for another couple of years at the very least.' He shook his head emphatically as she opened her mouth to respond. 'It isn't open to debate. *I'll* decide what's best for her.'

Lauren clamped down hard on the retort that rose all too readily to her lips, turning away to conceal her frustration. 'You've made that very clear,' she said.

Kerry's disgruntled return to the room put an end to any reply he might have been about to make. She certainly didn't need make-up to enhance her looks, but that wasn't the point of the exercise, Lauren knew.

What she wanted was what all young teenagers wanted—to look more adult.

The musical Brad had chosen was enjoyable enough to lift any mood. Kerry had thawed considerably by the interval, and completely by the end of the show.

'You're still a fuddy-duddy though,' she said in the restaurant he took them to for a late supper. 'I bet Mom would have let me wear make-up.'

'I very much doubt it,' Brad returned equably. 'She hardly ever wore any herself.' He looked across at Lauren, lips tilting. 'Still mad at me?'

'What gave you the idea I was mad at you?' she queried.

'The knife in my back might have a bearing.'

Her smile was involuntary. 'You were a bit bombastic.'

'When?' asked Kerry.

'While you were scrubbing your face,' he said. 'Lauren thinks you should be allowed a splash of lipstick.'

'I actually said a touch,' Lauren corrected. 'Not that you really need it.'

'Which brings us back to square one. How long is it going to take for those streaks to grow out?' Brad added.

'Ages.' Kerry sounded faintly defiant again. 'I could always have the rest done to match—or even shave it all off!'

His lips twitched. 'That might be a bit of an overkill, don't you think?'

'Lauren?' A woman detached herself from a small group about to pass their table. 'Is it really you?'

Lauren found her voice with an effort, the bottom

dropped right out of her stomach. 'Hello, Maureen. How are you?'

'Fine. Just fine! And how are you?'

'Great.' Smile fixed, Lauren glanced across at Brad. 'Maureen and I were at school together.'

'A lot of years ago,' laughed the other. Her gaze went from his face to Kerry's and back to Lauren's. 'Family outing, is it?'

'Mr Laxton's my employer.' Lauren wished the floor would open up and swallow her. 'This is his daughter.'

'You're a nanny?'

'Lauren's my companion,' said Kerry on a frosty note. 'I'm way past needing a nanny!'

'Debatable at times,' Brad put in drily. 'It's a rare coincidence you running into each other like this after so long.'

'Isn't it though?' Maureen agreed. 'When did you come back from Canada, Lauren?'

'Recently.'

'For good?'

'That's right.'

'Lucky you to fall straight into a job! We should get together some time.'

'I'm only in town for a couple of days,' Lauren said swiftly.

'I think your friends are getting a bit impatient,' Brad advised.

Maureen glanced towards the group hovering by the restaurant doors, then back again via a lingering, speculative look at Kerry to Lauren, obviously reluctant to leave it at that. 'Nice seeing you again, anyway.'

'You too,' Lauren lied.

She drew a shallow breath as the other woman moved on, conscious of Brad's eyes on her.

'I gather you were none too keen on the idea of getting together again,' he said.

'We weren't exactly close friends,' she returned. 'I didn't see much point.'

'No one you might *like* to look up while you're in the area?'

'I don't think so.' She kept her tone as casual as possible. 'It's all a long time ago.'

He said no more, to her relief. Running into Maureen Shelby had been bad enough. It was true that they'd never been close friends, but she'd known about the pregnancy, *and* the adoption. Everyone had known! From the way she'd looked at Kerry just now, there was a chance that seeds of suspicion, no matter how faint, could have been sown. Her own obvious disruption hadn't helped.

'So, what are we doing tomorrow?' asked Kerry. 'I suppose you'll be busy again, Dad?'

'Afraid so,' he said. 'Steve can deal with whatever crops up after that though. I thought we might hop across to Brittany for a few days.'

'Great!' she exclaimed.

'We didn't bring the right clothes for that kind of trip,' said Lauren, bemused by the suggestion.

'What we don't have we can get there,' Brad rejoined easily. 'It's a very casual place.'

'Mom loved it.' Kerry sounded reminiscent. 'We used to go there a lot when I was little. Can we have a *gîte*?'

'Might be difficult to find one going spare this time of year, but we can certainly try.' His attention was still on Lauren. 'Having doubts?'

It wasn't doubt she was feeling, just regret for the

years she'd been denied. 'None at all,' she said, brightening both voice and expression. 'It sounds wonderful!'

It was obvious that he wasn't completely convinced by the act, but he let it go. She had to stop dwelling on what was past and gone, and concentrate on making the most of what was still to come, she thought resolutely.

It was coming up to half-past twelve when they made it back to the flat. Almost asleep on her feet, Kerry went straight off to bed.

'I think I'll turn in too,' Lauren declared. 'It's been a long day.'

'A few more minutes won't hurt.' Brad indicated the sofa set within the curve of the huge window looking out over the darkened river. 'One or two things we should perhaps talk about.'

Lauren took a seat, steeling herself for whatever was to come. He sat down close though not too close, studying her for an endless moment before speaking.

'Seeing that woman back there in the restaurant upset you, didn't it?'

Denying it would be a waste of time and breath, she thought hollowly. What she had to find was a plausible reason for the reaction he'd by no means been blind to.

'Being uprooted from everything takes some getting over,' was all she could come up with. 'It just brought it all back, that's all.'

'There were no relatives you could have stayed with at the time?'

'No.'

'Not even grandparents?'

'They were all dead by then.' Lauren felt bound to offer more than just that bare statement. 'My mother was thirty-nine when I was born, my father forty.

They'd never really wanted a child at all. Dad's retired now, of course.'

'They've never wanted to come back home?'

'Not even for a visit.' She hesitated before seizing the opportunity. 'I'd as soon just tell them I'm getting married and leave it at that. They wouldn't come over anyway.'

It was difficult to tell what Brad's thoughts might be. 'Whatever you think best,' he said. There was another pause, a slight change of tone. 'Anything else to tell me?'

Lauren felt the band about her chest tighten almost unbearably. To have it all out in the open would be such a relief, but she dared not take the risk.

'Nothing I can think of,' she said, wondering how she could sound so calm about it with every nerve in her body on edge. She sought a change of subject. 'Will this be the first time you've been back to Brittany?'

'Since Claire died, you mean?' He sounded quite matter-of-fact about it. 'Yes, as it happens.'

'Won't you find it a bit too...nostalgic?'

'Nostalgia doesn't have to be sorrowful.' He drew her to him, smoothing the ball of his thumb gently across her lips. 'Kerry would have made it plain enough if she didn't want you with us.'

'I suppose.' Her eyes were luminous. 'We do seem to be getting on rather well.'

'Better than I could have hoped. Especially in so short a time.' He smiled. 'I think you cast a spell on the two of us.'

Hopefully a lasting one, she thought as he kissed her.

They parted for the night with reluctance on both sides. Lauren wondered if it had occurred to him that discretion would be the order of the day in Brittany too.

If they were to present Kerry with the news in two weeks' time, it was obviously going to be necessary to build an attachment between the two of them, but it must be done with finesse. Even then, the chances of her taking it well had to be remote.

Despite the summer crowds, they managed to find a *gîte* for rent in a small village on the west coast. Sleeping up to six people, it was larger than Lauren would have anticipated, comprising two bedrooms, a basic but adequate kitchen and a huge living area. With a little cove few people appeared to have discovered within walking distance, it offered almost everything anyone could wish for in her estimation.

They did their own cooking, having stocked up with groceries at the port. Brad proved a virtuoso on the barbecue. If Kerry was reminded of days gone by, she showed no sign of being upset by the memories.

For Lauren, the whole experience was pure paradise. This was the kind of family life she had dreamt about all these years. She wished they could stay here forever.

'Even this could pall after a while,' Brad observed when she said as much to him as they lounged on the beach the second morning. 'We need the mundane for contrast.'

'I'd hardly call your lifestyle mundane,' she returned lightly.

'Neither would I,' he agreed. 'I was speaking generally. I hope you're not having any second thoughts about putting Kerry in day school, by the way, because I've already made the arrangements.'

Eyes seeking the pretty young figure down by the water's edge, Lauren shook her head. 'She hates going away and leaving everything. Especially now she's met

Adrian and Co.' She stole a sideways glance at the bare-chested man propped comfortably against a rock, senses stirring as always. 'There'll be a price to pay, of course. She'll expect to have them all over to the house.'

'More your province than mine,' came the unperturbed reply.

'Do you plan on spending a lot of time away from home?' she asked after a moment.

'No more than necessary.' His tone had sharpened a fraction. 'I hope you're not thinking of suggesting I give it all up?'

'No, of course not. Lovely as it is, you'd die of boredom stuck at Ravella all the time.'

'At least I wouldn't be suffering the same kind of withdrawal symptoms. I know this was my suggestion, but much more of it and I'm going to blow a gasket!'

'Forbearance is good for the soul,' Lauren returned blandly.

'It isn't my soul I'm concerned with right now.' His gaze roved her body in the skimpy yellow bikini, his expression leaving little doubt of his feelings. 'Enough to drive a man to drink!'

'It's no easier for me,' she murmured. 'Sharing a room with Kerry is great, but I'd sooner be with you.'

'I should hope so too!' He paused. 'You think these last few days have helped the two of you get a bit closer?'

'In some ways, yes, though there's still a long way to go.'

'You'll get there. She certainly seems a lot happier.'

More to do with having him around than herself, she thought. No matter how close she and Kerry might get in time, it stood to reason that he would always mean the most.

Kerry came back up the beach, the look she rested on the pair of them impatient. 'How long are you two going to stay talking?' she demanded. 'The sea's warm as toast!'

Brad got lithely to his feet, swinging her up over a shoulder to the tune of her squeals. 'We'll see how warm you think it is when I dump you in it!'

Lauren watched him race down the stretch of sand to do as he had threatened, aware of smiles on the faces of others in the vicinity as they watched too. His relationship with Kerry was so different from what she had first believed. How could she ever have accused him of not caring?

That week was the happiest of her life. The three of them went everywhere together. If Kerry resented her presence at all, she certainly didn't show it.

'At least you know how to have fun!' she said magnanimously one night.

'Not *too* old, then?' Lauren queried, dodging the pillow that came winging across from the other bed.

'Quiet in there!' Brad called from next door. 'Some of us are trying to get some sleep!'

'Some of us need it more than others,' Kerry called back cheekily, raising a short laugh.

He was suffering the same frustrations she was suffering, Lauren knew. She longed to be with him, but Kerry was too light a sleeper to take the risk of creeping through later. They had the rest of their lives to make up for it anyway. A thought she clung to happily.

It had to come to an end eventually, of course. She said goodbye to the *gîte* with regret on Sunday morning. Apart from the necessary discretion, it had been a wonderful few days. Back at Ravella the same problems awaited. However well she and Kerry seemed to be doing, there was no way the news was going to be acceptable just yet—if at all.

They arrived at the house around four on the Monday afternoon. Kerry went straight over to the stables the moment they got in. She reappeared an hour later looking, to Lauren's eyes at least, as though she might have been crying.

Diamond had been well taken care of, she responded shortly when asked. They all had.

Whatever had happened, Lauren was pretty sure it had something to do with Mick. She considered confiding in Brad, but feared his reaction. She had to find some way of broaching the subject with Kerry herself.

She got her chance when Brad retired to the study after dinner to catch up on his e-mails, although it wasn't easy to get to the truth. It was only when she actually mentioned Mick's name that the floodgates finally opened. Kerry had found him in the tack room with a girl, it appeared. From the sound of it, they'd been pretty well advanced.

Lauren's first reaction was relief. She'd visualised even worse. 'I can appreciate how you feel,' she said carefully. 'I was let down by the first boy I fell for.'

Kerry raised a woebegone face. 'You were?'

'Yes. It devastated me too.' She paused, longing to put her arms about the girl; knowing it would probably be the last thing she wanted right now. 'Did they know you saw them?'

'No, they were too busy.'

Lauren could imagine. 'Your father will fire him when he hears about it,' she said.

The hazel eyes darkened. 'I don't want Dad to know!'

'He doesn't have to know how you feel about Mick, only what you caught him doing. It's more than sufficient reason.'

'But then there'll be nobody to look after the horses.'

They'd be able to do that themselves, it was on the tip of Lauren's tongue to say, but that would call for explanations she wasn't yet ready to give.

'It shouldn't be difficult to find someone to take his place,' she substituted.

Kerry looked torn between two fires. 'The horses are used to him. He's the only one apart from Dad who Caliph takes any notice of. Who's going to keep him exercised when Dad's away?'

Something she certainly couldn't take on, Lauren acknowledged. 'But how are you going to feel if he stays?' she asked.

Resolution firmed the young lips. 'I don't care any more. He isn't worth it.' She got to her feet. 'I'm going to bed.'

Lauren refrained from pointing out that it was only nine o'clock. At least her disillusionment over Mick had removed one concern. A quiet word in his ear should take care of the rest.

Brad returned with the unwelcome news that he had to go up to town the following day.

'I'll be back Wednesday,' he promised. 'We'll have the whole weekend to break the news to Kerry.' He paused, eyeing her consideringly. 'What kind of a wedding would you have in mind?'

'I hadn't thought that far,' Lauren admitted. 'Nothing elaborate for certain.'

Brad made no attempt to conceal his relief. 'I was hoping you would want something intimate.'

'The reason most people put on a show is to suit

others,' she returned lightly. 'We'll just be suiting ourselves.' She hesitated before continuing. 'Is it really so
necessary to rush things, Brad? We know how we feel
about each other, but Kerry can hardly be expected to
give us her blessing. Not at this juncture, anyway.'

He regarded her in silence for a moment, the expression in his eyes difficult to read. 'How long do you
think we should wait?' he asked at length in neutral
tones.

'Another couple of weeks at least.'

'You reckon that's going to make a difference?'

'It has to help.' Lauren made a small, appealing gesture. 'It isn't that I don't want to marry you, believe
me!'

'Just that you see Kerry's needs as greater than mine.'
He held up a staying hand as she made to reply. 'That
wasn't fair, I know. Her feelings have to be considered
too. All the same, it's only a month till the start of the
new term.' He shook his head decisively. 'No, she has
to be told this next weekend.'

He came over to where Lauren sat, drawing her to
her feet to take her face between his hands and bring
her mouth to his in a kiss that claimed possession in no
uncertain terms.

'There's nothing going to come between us!' he declared roughly when he came up for air at last.

Nothing he need ever know about, Lauren reassured
herself, unable to hold out any further against her own
yearning to be with him openly. With this man, and her
daughter, she had everything she could possibly want
in the world!

Informed at breakfast of her father's coming departure, Kerry showed surprisingly little reaction. She was
still recovering from the trauma of finding her hero had

feet of clay, Lauren took it. Some time today she would find a moment to have that quiet word with the young man. What he got up to in his own time was his business, but the stables was no place for a lovers' tryst.

Kerry didn't show up to see Brad off. Lauren did it with circumspection just in case they were under surveillance, watching the car disappear round the curve in the drive with a sense of deprivation. It wasn't just the lovemaking she was going to miss him for either. Without him, the house seemed so empty.

This was how Kerry must have felt the times in past holiday periods when he'd gone away and left her in Mrs Perriman's charge, she mused. Good as the woman was, she was no substitute for a parent. At least that would never happen again.

There was still no sign of her daughter when she made her way to the stables. She found Mick in the process of mucking out Caliph's stable.

'What's it to you?' he demanded when she mentioned the previous afternoon's incident. 'You've no more authority here than I have.'

'I'm in charge of a thirteen-year-old girl who shouldn't be subjected to the kind of scene you and your girlfriend were creating,' Lauren rejoined levelly.

'I didn't realise she was around,' he said. 'Anyway, it might stop her giving me the eye. She's a good-looking kid. It hasn't been all that easy holding her off!'

Green eyes blazed. 'From what I've seen, you've given her a great deal too much encouragement! Amusing, is it, to have a young girl worshipping at your feet?'

'Makes a change from this,' indicating the pile he'd just raked out from the stable. 'Anyway, I never touched her.'

'You'd better not either!' Lauren flashed. 'From now

on, you treat her with the respect due to her as your employer's daughter. And you keep your love life away from here too—if you don't want Mr Laxton to hear what you get up to on his property.'

Mick's face hardened. 'Are you threatening to tell him?'

'Only if I have cause to.' Lauren refused to be intimidated. 'The two of us will be taking a ride this afternoon. Just remember what I've told you.'

She turned away before he could make any response, heading back the way she had come. Kerry probably wouldn't thank her for putting her oar in, but she wouldn't know if Mick played his part. He'd certainly better!

It was gone ten when Kerry put in an appearance again. She agreed without much enthusiasm to a game of tennis, recovering her spirits once on the court.

'You're good, but I'm better!' she chortled on the way back to the house, having won two games out of three.

'Youth will out,' rejoined Lauren laughingly, and received an indulgent glance.

'You're not *so* old, I suppose.' There was a pause, a sudden change of tone. 'Didn't you ever want to get married?'

Lauren steadied her voice. 'Wanting isn't always enough.'

'You mean nobody ever asked you to marry them?'

'Nobody I could contemplate spending the rest of my life with.'

'It isn't too late to find somebody you could though, is it?'

'Well, no, I suppose not.' Lauren was cautious, not

about to jump to any conclusions through sheer wishful thinking.

'Dad too, I suppose.'

Lauren kept the rein tight. 'I thought you hated the thought of him getting married again?'

'It might be OK with somebody I liked. It's only a month till I go back to school,' she added obliquely.

Lauren wanted suddenly to laugh. 'A lot can happen in a month,' she said. 'Just look at what we've managed to pack into the last two weeks!'

From the expression on her daughter's face, that wasn't quite the response she was looking for, but she let the subject drop. Lauren hoped she wasn't reading too much into what had been said.

The day went through its phases. Kerry treated Mick with polite disdain when they went to ride in the afternoon, and seemed happy enough afterwards. Lauren waited until five to make a call to her parents, receiving the anticipated cool response.

'You do as you see fit,' said her mother. 'As you always did.'

Hardly always, it was on the tip of Lauren's tongue to retaliate, but she bit it back. There was no point in being bitter about what was past and gone. She was starting a new life now.

Brad rang at six. He had a business dinner to attend, he said, and might not get an opportunity later. Lauren thought about mentioning what Kerry had said earlier, but decided against it on the grounds that she might still be mistaken.

'I wish you were here!' she exclaimed impulsively, and sensed his smile.

'So do I. One night wasn't nearly enough to make up for a whole week of deprivation.'

'Is sex all you think about?' she asked teasingly.

'No,' he returned without haste. 'I already said, there's a whole lot more to you than that. As I hope you find in me too. I love you, Lauren.'

'I love you too,' she whispered.

His laugh was low. 'I'll see you tomorrow. Early as I can make it.'

Kerry was standing in the sitting-room doorway when Lauren turned. It was difficult to tell what she might be thinking.

'That was Dad, wasn't it?' she said.

There was no point in prevarication. Lauren made a wry gesture. 'It was, yes.'

'You said you loved him *too*, so he must have said it first.'

'I suppose he must.'

Kerry's expression still gave little away. 'Are you going to get married?'

'Yes.' Lauren held her breath for the response, letting it out on a relieved sigh as the young face broke into a smile.

'So you won't be leaving when I go back to school!'

'No. And you won't be going back to school,' Lauren added, seeing no reason to keep that a secret any longer. 'Not the same one, anyway. You'll be starting the autumn term at Brookfields.'

'Really and truly?' Kerry looked as if all her birthdays had come at once. 'And I'll be living here at home all the time?'

'Where else would you live?' Lauren was smiling too, glad to have it all out in the open—at least this part of it. 'You don't mind?'

'About you and Dad?' She shook her head. 'I might have at first, but not any more. Especially,' she added with a gamine grin, 'now I'll be going to Brookfields! I'm going to text Adrian!'

She'd departed before Lauren could say anything more. So much for all her concern, she reflected. She considered calling Brad back with the news, but decided it would be best left until his return, when they could start making plans.

Standing here in the house she would soon be mistress of, she found it hard to believe that little more than a couple of weeks had passed since the day she'd arrived on the doorstep. Two weeks to fall head over heels in love!

Far less than that in fact. She'd known almost immediately that here was the man she had been looking for all her adult life. If it weren't for the secret gnawing away inside her, she would be in seventh heaven right now.

CHAPTER NINE

ASSURED by Kerry that she was totally in favour, Brad lost little time in making arrangements for the wedding, seizing a cancellation at the register office in Stratford for the following Thursday. Lauren was left breathless by the speed of it all.

Sparked off by Adrian, via Kerry, the news went through the village like wildfire. His mother rang to extend her best wishes, and to say that Kerry was welcome to stay at the farm if they wanted to get away for a few days after the wedding. Lauren hadn't even considered that far ahead, and doubted if Brad would want to take the time, but she thanked the woman for the thought.

Brad, as it turned out, *had* thought that far ahead, with a cruise of the Norwegian fiords already booked. Mrs Perriman had agreed to take care of Kerry while they were gone, but he considered the offer to have her at the farm a better solution all round.

'More fun for her, and I know the Harrises will take care of her,' he said.

Lauren put up no arguments. Much as she loved her daughter, the thought of a few days on their own was heavenly.

Try as she might to keep unwelcome thoughts at bay, the deception haunted her. Her only comfort was the possibility that some time in the future, when the three of them were well and truly established as a family, she might find the courage to bring out the truth. It would

142

be a shock even then, but at least she would have proved just how much they meant to her.

She'd believed herself outwardly serene at any rate, but Brad sensed some discord.

'Want to talk about whatever's bothering you?' he asked when they took a stroll in the grounds after dinner one evening.

'Pre-wedding nerves, I suppose,' Lauren prevaricated.

Brad stopped walking to draw her close, hands supporting the back of her head as he looked down into her face. 'Is it because I've done all this before?'

'No.' She didn't have to lie on that score. 'It's just been so quick.'

He smiled. 'Do you doubt my feelings for you?'

'No.' She could say that with truth too for now. What she doubted was his ability to sustain those same feelings if her deception came to light too soon.

'I'm just a bit jittery, that's all,' she claimed, thrusting the thought aside once more. 'I'll be fine once it's all over.'

Whether he believed her or not, he let the subject drop. Continuing their stroll, with his arm about her shoulders, Lauren vowed for the umpteenth time to concentrate on the here and now instead of worrying about what might never happen. She was so lucky to have all this!

Not that Ravella would mean anything to her without Brad. There was no place on earth that could mean anything to her without him.

Kerry insisted on coming with her on the Tuesday to choose her wedding outfit.

'Too boring!' she declared to every garment Lauren selected as a possibility. 'Just because you're not getting married in church, you don't have to look as if you're going to the office!' She took a bright red dress with a short swirly skirt down from the rail, holding it up against Lauren to judge the length. 'This would look terrific! You've got great legs!'

'Thanks, but I think I'd prefer to see a little less of them,' Lauren returned drily.

'I bet Dad wouldn't. He hasn't been able to keep his eyes off you since the day you arrived!'

Lauren gave her a swift glance, relieved to see the sparkle in the hazel eyes. 'Rubbish!' she said.

'It's true. I'm not dense. Why do you think I was so rotten to you at first? I'm not nearly as bratty as I made out. I just wanted you to go.'

'But not any more?'

'Well, of course not. I'd still be stuck at Thurston for one thing. Anyway, Dad wasn't going let you go, was he?'

'You really don't mind any more?' Lauren ventured. 'About his getting married again? I know I can never take your mother's place.'

'Mom would have liked you,' came the reassuring response. 'She made Dad laugh a lot too. It used to be great when we were all together—just like it was in Brittany.'

'There'll be plenty more good times to come,' Lauren promised, moved beyond measure. 'Do you think you're too old for another visit to Disneyland? I've never been, you see.'

'If you're not, *I'm* definitely not!' Kerry sounded enthused. 'When?'

'Maybe half-term?'

'Great! Adrian and Sarah can come too!'

Lauren caught back the exclamation hovering on her

lips, aware of having dropped herself well and truly into that one. What Brad would think of the idea she didn't care to contemplate.

With Kerry still giving the thumbs-down to her more conservative choices, she settled in the end on a compromise in the shape of a knee-length, figure-skimming dress and floaty overwrap in deep blue silk, finishing off with a frivolous little hat covered in flowers all the colours of the rainbow.

'I still think Dad would like the red one best,' said Kerry on emerging from the shop, 'but it's your day. How about chocolate eclairs for tea?' she added, abandoning the wedding as a topic. 'They have scrumptious ones at the café over there!'

A teenager in years, but still a child at heart, thought Lauren smilingly, following her across the road.

She said as much to Brad that evening as they lingered over coffee.

'Betwixt and between,' he agreed. 'I'm lucky you're so willing to take her on. Not all women would be.'

Other women didn't have the same incentive, Lauren thought, feeling her spirits dip a little at the reminder. Not that she would have been reluctant to do it even if Kerry wasn't her daughter. Feeling the way she did about Brad, she'd have taken anything on.

As she looked at him now, hair ruffled by the light breeze, face and body relaxed, it was still difficult to believe that in another forty or so hours he would be her husband; still difficult to believe that any of this was really happening, in fact. Three weeks this coming Friday, that was all it had been. Three weeks in which her life had changed beyond recognition.

Her gaze dropped from the strong features, down the bronzed column of his throat revealed by the open shirt

collar, as she visualised the way in which the triangle
of dark hair on view at present exploded across his
chest, narrowing to a single line down the middle of the
muscular midriff to widen out once more about the masculine shape. A fine figure of a man in any language: a
man who meant everything to her.

She felt the colour come up in her cheeks on realising
she was under surveillance herself. Brad was smiling,
brows lifted quizzically.

'If ever there was a boost to the male ego, it's to see
that look in a woman's eyes,' he murmured.

'If ever there was a boost *needed* to the male ego!'
she retorted, collecting herself. 'I was simply wondering
what you were planning to wear on Thursday. After all,
we have to...' She broke off, abandoning the pretence.
'Is it too early to go to bed?'

'Shameless hussy!' he said, but he was already on his
feet.

The weather held up for the wedding. Standing at
Brad's side in the sunlit register office, Lauren spoke
the vows that made them husband and wife, closing her
mind to any intruding thoughts.

A fine-looking pair altogether, declared Mrs P, who'd
been thrilled to be asked to stand as a witness. Lauren
suspected she regarded herself as the one who'd brought
the two of them together.

Brad's second in command, Steven Dexter, had
driven up to be best man, accompanied by a small con-
tingent of people Brad counted as friends. There were
a few people from the area too—the Harris family
among them.

The reception was held back at Ravella. Lauren was

returning from the cloakroom when she overheard Kerry talking to Adrian.

'Sarah will be furious when she gets back and hears what she's missed!'

'You really don't mind, then?' he asked. 'Your dad getting married again, I mean?'

'Not when it means I don't have to go back to boarding-school. Lauren's OK, anyway.'

'But she's not like a real mother.'

The answer was forceful. 'I don't want a *real* mother.'

Lauren forced herself to move out of earshot, blinking fiercely at the prickling of tears behind her eyes. That hadn't been a slur against her personally, only against the woman Kerry believed had abandoned her. One thing was clear: she must never know they were the same person.

Deep in conversation with Neil Harris, Brad broke off to smile at her as she came up. The blue eyes narrowed a fraction as they rested on her face.

'Everything all right?' he asked.

Lauren summoned a smile of her own. 'Absolutely! The caterers certainly did a brilliant job at such short notice!'

'I doubt if Mrs P will give them top marks,' he said humorously. 'She was well and truly torn between being a witness and staying back here to see to everything herself.' He glanced at his watch. 'Anyway, we should be thinking about getting off.'

'Don't worry about Kerry while you're away,' said Neil. 'We'll look after her.'

'It's really good of you,' Lauren returned.

'No problem at all. She'll be company for Adrian. He gets a bit lonely sometimes, being an only child.'

Kerry seemed destined to remain one herself, thought Lauren. Much as she would love to have his child, a baby would hardly help matters.

They took their leave of everyone on the forecourt, with Kerry showing little concern over being left. Mrs P wiped a tear from her eye when Lauren impulsively kissed her.

'I can't tell you how happy I am for you both!' she said. 'It's like a fairy tale come true!'

'And they all lived happily ever after,' Brad quipped in the car. He glanced Lauren's way, the smile lingering about his lips. 'How do you feel?'

'Married,' she said, tongue-in-cheek. 'How do you feel?'

'I'd prefer to show you,' he responded with a glint. 'Later.'

'I can hardly wait,' she said, and meant it. To be together for the first time as man and wife would be wonderful!

The ship was no run-of-the-mill cruise liner, but a luxuriously appointed yacht carrying no more than forty passengers in total. Lauren was bowled over by their stateroom with its double bed and superb decor, the spacious, beautifully fitted bathroom and separate living area.

'It's like something out of a brochure!' she exclaimed.

'It *is* out of a brochure,' Brad returned, amused by her wide-eyed enthusiasm. 'We'll be sailing in a few minutes. Did you want to go up on deck?'

About to say yes, she took a look at him and changed her mind. 'I'd far rather stay here,' she said softly.

The blue eyes held a small, familiar flame. 'You'll not mind missing dinner?'

She laughed by way of response, holding out her arms. 'Try me.'

She'd thought it impossible to better what they'd already experienced together, but she was proved wrong. Brad took her to heights she couldn't have conceived. She gave herself to him wholly and completely, loving his mastery. He was all man, and he was all hers. Could any woman be luckier than she was?

The cruise itself was idyllic, the scenery out of this world. With more crew than clientele, the service on board was outstanding too. Lauren only had to lift a finger to have a steward hovering at her elbow.

She hadn't realised how well known Brad's face was to certain sections of the public via media coverage of his various business exploits. He was recognised by several people, and even approached by one man with a proposition, to which he responded with polite but firm uninterest.

'It might have been better if we'd gone somewhere totally private,' he said ruefully when the man had departed. 'Sorry about that.'

'It doesn't matter,' Lauren assured him. 'Not to me. I'm just beginning to discover how accomplished a husband I've got!'

'Only beginning?' he teased. 'I can see I'll have to improve my technique.'

He took her to a whole new plane again that night. 'Like riding the biggest roller coaster in the world!' she murmured after the final, shattering climax. 'You're phenomenal!'

Brad's laugh was soft. 'You'd inspire any man!' He waited a moment or two, his tone altered when he spoke again. 'How would you feel about having a child of our own?'

Lauren's heart missed a beat. 'You said the patter of little feet held little appeal for you,' she got out.

'I probably meant it at the time, but I'm beginning to have second thoughts,' he admitted.

'What about Kerry?' she asked. 'Mightn't she feel pushed out?'

'It would be up to us to make sure she didn't.' He lifted his head to search her face. 'Don't you want a baby?'

'I'd love one,' she declared. 'I just…'

'Kerry will be OK,' he said. 'Anyway, it might not even happen.' His eyes glinted. 'We can enjoy trying though. Starting right now, in fact!'

Lauren gave in to the emotion sweeping her without further struggle. To have a child with Brad would be wonderful! Right now, she couldn't think of anything else.

The ten days passed all too quickly. The pouring rain and howling gale that greeted them back in England was hardly scheduled to cheer any spirits. It took Kerry to do that, with a welcome home that set Lauren's heart aglow.

'It's been great at Adrian's,' she said, 'but I've really missed our rides together. And the tennis. Adrian doesn't play nearly as well as you. It's boring winning *all* the time!'

'Great oaks from little acorns grow!' commented Brad drily. 'If the wind changes you'll stay like that,' he added as she stuck out her tongue at him. 'Adrian would go a bundle on you then.'

'Adrian's just a friend, not a boyfriend,' came the

lofty response. 'I'm steering clear of those until I'm older.'

Brad lifted an eyebrow at Lauren as she departed. 'You reckon she means it?'

'For now.' Lauren briefly contemplated telling him about Mick, deciding against it because there really wasn't all that much to tell. 'I suppose I'd better go and start unpacking,' she said instead. 'At least I don't have all the washing and ironing to think about—although I could give Mrs P a hand.'

Brad laughed. 'She'd throw a fit if you even offered. I'll start catching up on some correspondence.'

There was certainly enough of it piled on the hall table, with probably a good deal more awaiting his attention in the study. He'd be heading for town at the earliest, Lauren assumed. After ten days away, there'd be a lot needing his attention.

He went the following morning. Something she had to get used to, Lauren knew, but she missed him dreadfully.

With less than three weeks to go now before the start of the new term, there was no shortage of things for her to do too. The rest of Kerry's belongings had to be fetched from Cambridge, and the new uniform bought, for a start.

Her relationship with her daughter improved by the day. Mrs P was moved to remark on the change in Kerry's whole attitude.

'It's what she's missed so badly,' she said. 'Mr Bradley's done his best, but a girl needs a mother to talk to. Especially now at her age.'

Something she'd missed herself, thought Lauren wryly. Her mother had never been very approachable.

She hoped Kerry would confide in her. Telling her about Mick had been a good start.

That young man appeared to have taken what she'd told him seriously. At any rate, he left Kerry well alone. If she had any lingering feelings for him, she showed no sign of it.

Brad returned at the weekend to a warm welcome from both of them.

'You've made such a difference to my life,' he said later when he and Lauren were alone. 'Kerry's too. She's a different girl!'

'As much down to Adrian and Co, and not having to go back to boarding-school,' Lauren depreciated.

'A part of it, maybe, but it's obvious how close the two of you are becoming. I doubt if she'll ever get used to calling you Mother though.'

'Claire was the only mother she ever knew,' she said, stifling the pang. 'I'm happy the way things are.'

The blue eyes kindled. 'Me too,' he said softly. 'Ecstatically!'

For how long? came the thought as he drew her to him. Was she living in a fool's paradise imagining she might be able to keep the secret forever?

Her response to his kiss was almost feverish in its intensity, arousing him to instant and devastating passion. Lauren wrapped her legs about the lean hips as they joined together, blotting out everything else.

They spent the weekend doing all the things families did together, finishing off with a barbecue on Sunday afternoon at Kerry's urging. The Harrises came, along with another two couples with children at Brookfields. Reticent at first, Lauren relaxed when it became evident that any curiosity the visitors might have about her was under wraps.

She was talking with Neil Harris when Mrs Perriman came out to say there was someone wanting to speak with her. Finding Maureen Shelby waiting in the sitting room was a shock that brought her heart leaping sickeningly into her throat.

'What are you doing here?' she asked. 'How did you even know where I was?'

'One of the people I was with that night recognised your Mr Laxton,' came the calm return. 'It wasn't too hard to find his out-of-town address. The housekeeper told me the two of you just got married. Congratulations!'

Lauren ignored the salutation, eyeing the other woman's sharpish-featured face with misgivings growing in her by the second. Maureen Shelby had been no real friend of hers in school, and was certainly not here in the name of friendship now.

'Just what do you want?' she demanded.

Maureen cast an appraising glance about the room before answering. 'I'd have thought it might be obvious. That girl who was with you that night is your daughter, isn't she?'

'Don't be ridiculous!' Lauren put everything she had into the scornful retort.

'It's the truth—although the thought might never have occurred to me if you hadn't looked so utterly distraught when you saw me. Anyone who knew you'd had a child *and* it had been adopted might have jumped to the same conclusion. The age was about right, the colouring very similar. Clever of you to find her after all these years. Even cleverer to inveigle her father into marrying you. Catch of the century, *he* has to be!'

She shook her head as Lauren began another refutation. 'You're wasting your time trying to deny it. If it wasn't true, you'd have called your husband in by now to throw me out. As you are still trying though, it's evident you haven't told him. That will be my pleasure if you don't come through.'

Lauren pulled herself together, acknowledging the uselessness of further protest. 'Come through with what exactly?'

'Money. What else? You've married into an abundance of it. It shouldn't be hard to lay your hands on enough to make *my* life a bit more comfortable. A couple of thousand would do. For a start, at any rate.'

'I don't have any money of my own.' Lauren did her best to sound positive. 'And blackmail carries a heavy penalty.'

'You won't be going to the law,' came the unmoved response. 'How you get the money is your concern, but I'm not leaving here without it.'

'What did I ever do to make you so vindictive?' Lauren burst out.

'Not a lot,' Maureen admitted. 'But this has nothing to do with the past. I'm simply taking advantage of a heaven-sent opportunity. I *need* money!'

'You could try earning it.'

'Oh, I have. Trouble is, I'm not all that keen on the nine-to-five routine. What I really fancy doing is swanning around the way you're going to be doing, but rich husbands don't grow on trees so I'll settle for what I can get.' She raised suggestive eyebrows. 'I hear you're having a barbecue. Aren't you going to invite me?'

Short of calling Brad in right now to learn the hard facts, Lauren was left with no choice. That Maureen meant what she said about not leaving the house empty-

handed, she didn't doubt for a moment. Her own money
had been transferred to an account with a Stratford
bank, and Brad had arranged a generous personal allow-
ance, but even if she could get to a machine to draw
cash today she would be limited to a few hundred
pounds, which was hardly going to satisfy her avaricious ex-schoolmate. Tomorrow was the earliest she
could lay her hands on the amount asked for, which
meant finding some reasonable excuse for Maureen to
stay overnight. Even then, it obviously wasn't going to
finish there.

It was all too much to handle at the moment, she
thought desperately. She needed time to think.

'You'd better come in, then,' she said with reluctance.

Brad was presiding over the grills, a glass of wine to
hand. His surprise on seeing the newcomer was evident.

'Maureen's touring,' Lauren announced in as light a
tone as she could manage. 'She called in to say hello.'

'I recognised who you were when we met, of course,'
Maureen cut in before he could say anything. 'I saw a
magazine article about Ravella last year, and I couldn't
resist taking a peep at the real thing while I'm in the
area. Hope you don't mind?'

'Not at all,' Brad returned courteously. 'Make yourself at home.'

'I intend to,' she said softly, turning away so that only
Lauren heard her. 'Right at home!'

For Lauren, the afternoon dragged interminably. She
was aware of Brad's eyes on her from time to time, and
knew he recognised her discomposure if no one else
did. Maureen herself was completely at ease, chatting
away happily with everyone. She took a special interest
in Kerry, who looked totally unimpressed.

People began leaving around six. By half-past, it was down to just the Harrises and Maureen. Lauren felt her spirits lift a fraction when the latter offered her thanks for a lovely afternoon and said her goodbyes, only to have the faint hope that the woman had changed her mind dashed when she reappeared to announce apologetically that her car had acquired two flat tyres during its stand out front.

'I can't imagine what can have caused it!' she deplored.

Lauren could. It would have taken no more than a couple of minutes to open up both valves. With no hope of getting anyone out to the car at this hour on a Sunday, Brad extended an immediate invitation to spend the night.

If the afternoon had dragged, the evening seemed to go on forever. Maureen angled unabashedly for a tour of the house after dinner. Brad did the honours himself, returning poker-faced. Maureen looked put out too.

'Bet she made a pass at him!' Kerry whispered to Lauren.

Brad confirmed the guess when they retired for the night, his opinion of the woman clear.

'She's out for whatever she can get,' he said grimly. 'I'd doubt very much if it was any spur-of-the-moment idea to call on you. I've a noon meeting, so I'll have to leave it to you to ring the garage in the morning. Just get rid of her as soon as you can.'

'I will,' Lauren promised, hoping she could. 'I'm sorry for landing you with her.'

'It's hardly your doing. You hadn't even seen her in years.'

'I know.' She made a helpless little gesture. 'I still

feel responsible for her being here.' She hesitated before saying it. 'She hasn't asked you for money?'

'No.' The blue eyes narrowed a fraction as he studied her. 'Has she asked you?'

There was only one answer she could give. 'No.'

'If she does, and you do, she'll be back for more,' he warned.

'I know,' she said again. 'Are you going to be gone all week?'

'I should be able to get back Wednesday.' Successfully sidetracked, he gave her a smile. 'Shall you miss me?'

'Like crazy!' Her voice shook a little. 'But you're worth waiting for.'

He responded with action as well as words, kissing her into blessed oblivion.

It didn't last, of course. Lying beside him later, listening to his steady breathing, she knew she should wake him now and tell him the truth rather than give in to Maureen's demands, but she still couldn't bring herself to do it.

Morning found her heavy-eyed and weary after a near-sleepless night. Maureen was still to show her face when Brad left at eight-thirty.

'Get rid of that woman as soon as you possibly can,' he reiterated on the doorstep. 'I'll ring you tonight.'

Mouth tingling from his parting kiss, Lauren turned back into the house to see Maureen standing bare feet away. Judging from her expression, she had overheard Brad's instruction.

Her first words confirmed it. 'You'll get rid of me when I've got money in my hand! The sooner you put it there, the better!'

'And after that?' Lauren asked.

'Depends how long I can make the first lot last.'

Lauren lifted an unsteady hand to push back the lock of hair fallen over her cheek, fighting for composure. 'You realise Brad wouldn't hesitate to call in the police if he knew what you were doing!'

'But he isn't going to know, is he? You're too scared of losing all this. Not that I can blame you for that.'

'Thanks.' Lauren kept the sarcasm low-key, too dispirited for any further attempt at intimidation. 'We have to drive into Stratford to the bank. It should be open by the time we get there.'

'Oh, I think breakfast first. The full works for me. It isn't often I get the chance to indulge.'

She'd be wasting her time refusing, Lauren knew. The other had her over a barrel.

Mrs Perriman made no attempt to conceal her disfavour when asked to produce a full English breakfast for the guest. Visitors, in her estimation, should stir themselves to attend meals with the regular household.

Lauren carried fresh coffee through to the small breakfast room herself. Already seated at the table set in the window, Maureen took up her cup with purposely extended little finger.

'Must remember I'm eating with the gentry now!'

Lauren let the sneer pass without comment. She poured coffee for herself, needing stimulation in order to get through the rest of this ordeal. She was being a fool going ahead with it, she knew.

'Don't look so glum,' Maureen advised. 'You're spoiling your looks. You wouldn't have got this far without them. Come to think of it,' she added, 'they're responsible for the whole caboodle. You'd better keep a sharp eye on that daughter of yours. She's going to be a man-catcher herself.'

More than could be said for her these days, Lauren thought, viewing the sallow face and limp dark hair badly in need of styling. It was almost laughable that she'd actually had the gall to try it on with Brad. He wouldn't have looked at her twice under any circumstances.

As if on cue, Kerry popped her head round the door, looking surprised to see the two of them seated there.

'I thought you'd gone already,' she said to Maureen.

'I haven't had breakfast yet,' the latter answered. 'You might go and give the housekeeper a gee-up. I'm starving to death here!'

A few weeks ago, Kerry might have felt moved to some pert retort. Today, she kept her mouth shut, directing a somewhat puzzled glance in Lauren's direction before going to do as she was bid—or so it was assumed.

Conversation—if it could be called that—lapsed. They were sitting there in silence when Mrs Perriman brought in the loaded tray. She said nothing either, though her expression spoke volumes. Lauren winged a mental apology, to be followed up with a verbal one at the first opportunity.

She phoned the local garage while Maureen was eating. Special equipment was needed to replace tyres on the spot, she was told. They'd send a low loader to collect the car. Meanwhile, there was the two thousand Maureen was demanding to be collected.

Standing there, visualising a future where such demands became a regular occurrence, Lauren knew a sudden fierce and final rejection. Giving in to blackmail was no way to live! Whatever the consequences, it was time she faced up to the woman in there.

She went back to the breakfast room, exerting every

ounce of will-power to keep herself on track. Maureen looked pointedly at her watch.

'They'll be open now. I think I'll have a walk round the grounds while you go and get the money.'

'I'm not going anywhere,' Lauren declared. '*You* are. They're sending transport for the car. You will go with it!'

Eyebrows plucked within an inch of their life drew together. 'You're in no position to turn me down. Not if you want to keep what you've got.'

'I'll take the risk.' Lauren was amazed by her own control. 'Do your worst!'

The sallow face had colour now, burning high on the cheeks. 'Oh, I will, don't doubt it! The whole sordid little story! Just imagine how your darling Kerry's going to feel when she hears who you really are!'

'What does she mean?' asked a voice, bringing both pairs of eyes swivelling to where Kerry stood in the doorway. 'What's she talking about, Lauren?'

CHAPTER TEN

MAUREEN got in before Lauren could draw breath, malice in both voice and face. 'I'm talking about the time you were born thirteen years ago to a sixteen-year-old schoolgirl! Do the arithmetic for yourself. You're bright enough!'

Kerry's eyes fixed on Lauren, bewilderment giving way slowly to devastated comprehension. 'You're my mother,' she whispered. 'My *real* mother!'

Lauren swallowed on the lump in her throat, hating herself even more than Maureen for creating this moment. 'Yes, I am,' she said thickly. 'I'm just sorry you had to find out this way.'

Eyes dark, Kerry gazed at her as if at a stranger. 'Does Dad know?'

Lauren shook her head, her stomach lurching at the expression that came over her daughter's face.

'You lied!' she burst out. 'Right from the start!'

'I know.' Lauren yearned to go to her. She didn't because she could guess what the reaction would be right now. 'I'm sorry,' she repeated helplessly. 'It was wrong of me to keep it from you. From both of you. I never intended things to happen the way they have.'

'Oh, I bet you didn't!' The hazel eyes were glittering—tears not far away. 'I'm going to ring him!'

She had turned tail and gone before Lauren could say another word. Not, she had to admit, that there was very much she could say.

'Still think it's worth the risk?' Maureen sneered.

Lauren looked at her with loathing. 'I want you out of here,' she said. 'Now!'

'I can't leave without the car,' the other pointed out.

'You can sit in it till they come for it,' Lauren returned hardly. 'Your things will be brought out to you. I'll have you forcibly removed from the house if necessary,' she added when the woman failed to stir herself. 'I've nothing to lose now, remember?'

'You've everything to lose when that husband of yours gets to hear the news,' Maureen retorted, but she got up. 'I'd like to be a fly on the wall when you try convincing *him* you never intended things to happen the way they did.'

It was going to be difficult, Lauren knew. If she'd lied about one thing, why not another? He was going to think what any man might think in the circumstances: that she'd inveigled him into marrying her as the only way she could be with her daughter. To say nothing of the other advantages.

He would still be on the road. Even if Kerry managed to reach him via his car phone, it would be a couple of hours before he could get back. Two hours in which to try getting through to her at least.

She asked one of the domestic helps to take Maureen's bag out to her, then went to seek her daughter. The bedroom door was locked against her. There was no response forthcoming to her appeal. Lauren kept up her efforts for several minutes, but it was hopeless.

The low loader arrived and, watching from a window, Lauren saw Maureen get into the cab with the driver. The woman was going to be faced with a hefty, and almost certainly unnecessary, bill for all this, but she deserved a great deal worse for what she'd attempted to do. The price she herself would have to pay was incalculable as yet.

She was attempting to calm herself via the piano when Brad eventually arrived. She saw the car draw up through the window; saw the look on his face when he got out and headed for the house. Fingers stiff and heavy, she stopped playing and lowered the lid over the keys, to sit waiting for whatever was to come.

Brad wasted neither time nor breath on entering the room. 'Is it true?' he demanded.

'Yes,' she said.

The blue eyes were icy cold, his jawline rigid. 'You scheming little bitch!' he jerked between his teeth.

'It wasn't like that!' she rejoined desperately. 'All I wanted in the beginning was to see her. The job was just too much of a temptation. I didn't anticipate falling in love with you.'

'I'm sure you didn't.' The sarcasm was biting. 'You played me for a fool!'

'No!' Lauren came to her feet, clutching at the piano for support. 'I never lied about the way I feel. Not at any time! I love you, Brad. You've got to believe that!'

'Like hell!' His back to the closed door, his face set in lines she'd never seen there before, he was formidable. 'I even caught a certain familiarity myself at times, but I failed to tie it down.' His laugh was brittle. 'Or maybe simply closed my mind to it. There's none so blind as those who don't want to see! I only...' He broke off, jaw clenching afresh. 'How did that woman find out about it anyway?'

'She knew I'd had a baby, and that the girl had been adopted. She put two and two together when she saw Kerry and me together that night at the restaurant.'

'Astute of her.' He paused. 'So she *was* after money.'

'Which I refused to supply, hence the spite.' Lauren's tone was flat, her emotions under strict control. 'I think you should go and see Kerry. She's in her room with the door locked. She won't speak to me.'

'Is there any wonder? You worm your way into her affections then drop this on her! How would you expect her to react?'

'The way she is doing, I suppose. For now, at any rate.'

'You reckon she's going to come round to the idea?'

'In time. If we handle it the right way.'

'There's no ''we'' about it,' he rejoined hardly. 'There are flights to Toronto every day. You'll take the earliest I can get a seat on.'

Lauren shook her head. 'I won't go.'

The hardened mouth tautened still further. 'You don't have a choice.'

'I'm your wife,' she pointed out. 'Try throwing me out, if you like, but I'm not leaving!

'Brad!' The momentary rage dissipated, she stretched an appealing hand as he started to turn away. 'Don't go—please!'

But he was already at the door, expression unrelenting. 'I'm going to see Kerry. She's the most important part of all this.'

Lauren stood motionless for several minutes after he'd gone, the desperation mounting in her. She'd brought this on herself, of course, but knowing it made it no easier to bear. Brad had to be made to listen to her—made to believe her. Kerry too. She loved them both to distraction. The thought of never seeing either of them again was too much to even contemplate.

She forced herself to move, not at all sure where she was going but unable to stay here in the room where

Brad had first kissed her any longer. He was coming back down the stairs as she emerged. Lauren's heart plunged like a stone on seeing the look on his face, their personal problems pushed aside by a sudden premonition of disaster.

'She's gone,' he clipped. 'At a guess, I'd say she's headed where she usually heads when she's upset—to Diamond.' He made a curt gesture as Lauren started forward. 'I'll go after her myself. You just hope she hasn't come to any harm!'

Lauren was still standing where he'd left her when Mrs Perriman came through from the rear.

'I thought I heard Mr Bradley's voice,' she said.

'Yes, he had to turn back.' Lauren could only wonder at the steadiness of her voice.

'Three for lunch, then?'

'I— Yes.' There was no other reply to be made. 'I'm not sure about dinner.'

'Plenty of time.' The housekeeper obviously sensed something not right, but she kept her own counsel.

Mind numb, Lauren took herself out to the terrace to watch for the two most important people in her life returning. The sky was overcast today, the cloud hanging grey and threatening. She couldn't have moved even if it had poured with rain.

How much time passed before she saw father and daughter emerging from the trees she couldn't have said. She got shakily to her feet as they mounted the steps, holding out her hands to the white-faced girl at Brad's side.

'Kerry, I'm sorry! I'm so sorry!' she choked.

Hatred blazed in the hazel eyes. 'Don't you come near me, you liar! I was right about you all along! You just wanted Dad's money!'

'I don't care about the money!' Lauren pleaded. 'I care about you! I've always cared about you!'

'If you did, you wouldn't have given me away!'

'I didn't have a choice. Not then. I—'

'You heard what she said.' Brad spoke in low tones. 'Leave her alone!'

Lauren resisted the urge to make any further appeal. It wasn't going to be any use. Not at present, anyway. Maybe later, when things had calmed down a little, she could try again. She *had* to keep on trying! Not just with Kerry, but with Brad too.

'Where did you find her?' she asked as her daughter stalked past her to head indoors.

'In Diamond's box,' he said. 'Lucky she hadn't taken off. The state she was in, anything could have happened.' His tone was unyielding, his jaw set. 'I meant what I said. You leave her alone. You gave up any rights thirteen years ago.'

Lauren kept her voice calm with an effort. 'I didn't give them up, they were taken from me. I was sixteen. What else could I have done?'

'There are societies unmarried mothers can turn to.'

'If I'd done that, look what she'd have missed out on. You and Claire gave her all the things I'd never have been able to give her.'

The blue eyes viewed her unwaveringly, the hardness in them undiminished. 'You think the material things are so all-important?'

'No.' She could see where he was heading. 'I meant what I said back there, Brad. I couldn't care two hoots about money! I married you because I love you! Because you're the only man I ever felt this way about!'

Dark brows lifted sardonically. 'Not even the father?'

'Especially not the father.'

'A bad lot, was he?'

'No. Just another misguided teenager. It was a party. We'd both had too much to drink.'

'So he got laid, and you got pregnant.' There was a brief pause, a change of tone. 'Where is he now?'

'Dead.' She said it unemotionally. 'He was killed ten years ago in a car accident. He came from a very good family, in case you're wondering.'

'Don't push it,' he advised grimly. 'I'm hanging on to my better nature by a thread to start with. We'd better get on in. Mrs P's going to be wondering what the hell's happening.'

Lauren accompanied him in silence. She had known it wasn't going to be easy, but it was proving harder than she'd even imagined. She had no intention of giving up though. However long it took to get through to them both, she was sticking with it.

Mrs Perriman met them in the hall. 'I've had lunch ready half an hour!' she complained. 'The salmon will be all dried up by now!'

'It'll be fine,' Brad answered. 'Just the two of us though. Kerry isn't feeling too well.'

Sympathy took over instantly from annoyance. 'Oh, the poor lamb! Is there anything I can take her?'

He shook his head. 'Best if she's left to sleep it off.'

'I'm not very...' Lauren began, voice fading away before the glance he turned her way.

'We'll be through in a minute or two,' he told the housekeeper.

'If you're staying, you'll carry on as normal,' he stated low-toned as the woman departed. 'This is a strictly private affair!'

'We're unlikely to keep it that way if both of you treat me as if I had the plague,' Lauren pointed out.

'Mrs P's no fool. If she doesn't sense something wrong already, she very soon will.'

'She can sense whatever she likes,' came the curt reply.

Lunch was an ordeal. The two of them conversed whenever the housekeeper was in the room, but Lauren couldn't have repeated a word of what was actually said. She could have been eating sawdust for all the taste that came through.

Suit jacket discarded, white silk shirt still pristine, Brad made her ache. She found herself watching his hands when he poured wine, remembering the feel of those long, tensile fingers: the lingering, tingling caresses. The mouth that had roved her whole body with such devastating passion was a thin straight line, his eyes like steel.

'We have to talk!' she said fiercely when Mrs Perriman had come and gone for the last time. 'You have to listen to me, Brad! I love you. There's nothing you can say or do that's going to alter that!'

Leaning back in his chair, glass in hand, he regarded her with irony. 'You'll be telling me next that staying with Kerry was the furthest thing from your mind when I asked you to marry me.'

Lauren took a grip on herself before answering. 'Of course it wasn't. It couldn't be. But I couldn't have accepted *just* for that reason. You knew how I felt about you. You had to know!'

'I knew I could satisfy you in bed.'

'It was more than that. A whole lot more! All right, I should have told you the truth at the start. I didn't because I was afraid you'd refuse to let me see Kerry. I'd have left when she went back to school if you hadn't—'

'If I hadn't let myself get carried away?' Brad interposed cynically. 'With that face and body you were halfway there the moment I opened the door to you. All you had to do was play me along. Your technique was admirable, I have to admit. You had me totally hoodwinked!'

Lauren gazed at him helplessly. Whatever she said, however hard she tried, she wasn't reaching him. She got to her feet, unable to take any more for the present.

'Stay away from Kerry,' he ordered. 'She's upset enough.'

'She's *my* daughter!' she flashed back.

'Only by birth.' He wasn't giving an inch. 'She'll decide for herself whether she wants to talk to you.'

Lauren left him sitting there, heading for the terrace again and fresh air. She should never have begun this, she thought hollowly. She should have let go a long, long time ago. All she'd done was cause disruption.

It was too late now for regrets. With Kerry due to start at Brookfields in a week, she had to carry on as intended. Given time to adjust, Kerry might eventually start to come round a little. Brad was another matter. His pride was at stake. Men set so much store by it.

At least, she consoled herself, things couldn't get any worse than they already were.

Kerry didn't put in an appearance all afternoon. Brad spent it in the study, emerging at six to go straight upstairs. It was a quarter to seven when he came down again, already changed for the evening. Only then did Lauren stir herself to follow suit.

Sharing a bedroom was going to be difficult enough while he continued to entertain the same view of her motives, she thought numbly on reaching it; sharing a bed was impossible. She gathered some things together and took them across to the room she had originally used.

Household linen was kept in a walk-in closet at the top of the back stairs. To reach it, she had to pass Kerry's door. It was firmly closed, with no sound issuing from within. Lauren bore down hard on the urge to try a further approach.

Far from hungry, but not about to stay out of sight, she put on the first things that came to hand to go down to dinner. The cream silk trousers and loose top looked a little overdressed for the occasion, but she couldn't be bothered changing again.

It was spot on the half-hour when she walked into the dining room, to find the two of them already seated. Kerry wouldn't even look at her as she took her place at the table. Lauren suspected it was only at Brad's insistence that she was here at all.

'Nice outfit,' he commented drily.

'Thank you,' she said expressionlessly.

'How can you talk to her?' Kerry burst out. 'She's no right to even be here!'

'But I *am* here, and I'm staying,' Lauren answered before Brad could speak. 'I'm not going to apologise again for what I did thirteen years ago, Kerry. What I can tell you is there hasn't been one day in those thirteen years when I haven't thought about you—wondering where you were, what you looked like, whether you were happy. I came to look for you because I couldn't stand not knowing any more.'

'Just how *did* you find us?' Brad cut in. 'The law says only the adopted child has a right to information.'

'I hired a private detective,' Lauren acknowledged. 'Don't ask me how he managed to obtain the detail he came up with because I've no idea. I paid him to do a job, and he did it.'

'Unlawfully!'

'I dare say. I didn't care *how* he did it.'

He regarded her coldly. 'A full case history, was it?'

'If you mean did I know before I came that you were one of the country's most successful businessmen, the answer is yes,' she said. 'It made no difference.'

He didn't believe her, it was evident. Neither, judging from her expression, did Kerry. Despite herself, Lauren felt her determination to stick it out beginning to slip a little.

'You'd come to like me before this happened,' she appealed to her daughter. 'I'm still the same person!'

'No, you're not,' came the unequivocal reply.

The sudden silence as Mrs Perriman appeared in the doorway could almost be felt. The housekeeper was certainly aware of some atmosphere in the room; her glance from one face to another was more than a little concerned. Lauren conjured a faint smile for her, though she doubted if it deceived her at all.

'Just eat,' Brad commanded when she'd gone. 'Anything else that has to be said can wait.'

Lauren applied herself to the stuffed avocados without appetite. She could feel her daughter's animosity coming across the table in waves. Perhaps when she remembered the new way of life she was due to start soon, she would realise things weren't all bad. It was clutching at straws, but what else was there?

Kerry disappeared again right after the meal, leaving the two of them to take coffee in the sitting room. Brad poured drinks, and put some music on, settling back on a sofa and closing his eyes as if in disinclination to discuss matters any further.

Lauren stood it as long as she could. But ignoring the subject wasn't going to help. She got up and went across to where he sat, kneeling on the cushion to put her lips to his with all the pent-up emotion of the last few hours.

His mouth remained passive, neither drawing away nor responding, though she felt the tension throughout his body. She gave up after a moment or two, sitting back to look at him helplessly.

'You really think it's all been an act?'

'The sex, no,' he said.

'It's more than just sex! You know it is!'

He studied her, taking in every detail of her face beneath the golden halo of her hair; shifting his gaze with deliberation down the length of her body, and back again. 'I don't *know* anything any more. Not where you're concerned. I believed you were genuine as they come!'

'Apart from this one thing, I am,' she pleaded. 'Be honest about it, Brad. If you'd known who I was that first day, would you have let me see Kerry?'

'Considering she'd never expressed any desire to meet her real mother, no,' he said. 'What I might have done was sound her out about it. It would have been her choice then, not yours.'

'I couldn't take the risk. I thought if I could only see her, even once, I'd have something to hold in my mind. She was just two days old when they took her from me. I didn't even have a photograph of her as a baby! Have you any idea what those first years were like?' Her voice was impassioned, eyelashes damp. 'Well, I'll tell you. They were hell! I hated my parents for not standing by me! I hated being uprooted from everything I'd ever known because they couldn't stand the gossip! Most of all, I hated myself for letting it happen!'

'That's a lot of hate,' he said. 'Do you still feel the same?'

Lauren shook her head, already ashamed of the outburst. 'I realised it wasn't helping anything. I trained in childcare to try and make up for what I'd lost. It helped a little.'

'What made you decide to search for her this particular year?'

'Realising she wasn't going to be a child for very much longer.' She made a small despairing gesture. 'I've blown it, haven't I?'

It was a moment or two before he answered, tone just a mite less chilly. 'Not necessarily. She's in shock right now. Give her time.'

Green eyes bored into blue, unable to penetrate the veil drawn over them. 'Do I have the time?'

His smile was thin. 'As you pointed out earlier, you're my wife. You have rights.'

'That was anger talking, not me.' Lauren hesitated, aware of treading on dangerous ground. 'If you want me to go, I will.'

The smile came again, no more mirthful than before. 'Putting the ball fairly and squarely in my court. No, dammit, I don't want you to go! If we don't have what I thought we had, we'll just have to make do with what there is.'

Lauren held back the protest that rose to her lips. No amount of verbal assurances were going to convince him. All she could do was show him how she felt.

'I moved my things out of our room,' she said, recollecting. 'I thought it was what you'd want.'

'Then you'd better move them back again.' He tossed

off the drink he was holding, and set down the glass. 'I've things to do.'

Lauren sat for several minutes after he'd gone from the room, trying to believe that everything would work out in the end. Brad still wanted her; that had to be a start. Whether Kerry would ever come to regard her in any better light again only time would tell.

She was in bed when Brad finally came up at midnight. He undressed without bothering to put on any lights, slinging his clothing across a chair and coming straight across to get between the cool cotton sheets.

Lauren turned to him eagerly, arms sliding over the broad naked shoulders, body moulding against him. His physical response was instant, the mouth seeking hers lacking nothing in passion. What was missing was tenderness, but she could hardly expect to regain everything all at once.

She put everything she knew into the following moments, kissing her way down the length of the hard masculine body to bring the breath hissing through his teeth at the sensations created by lips and tongue. When he turned her under him she was pliant in his hands, moist and welcoming. Feeling him there inside her, a part of her again, was sheer ecstasy.

The elation faded when he rolled away from her almost immediately after climaxing with a murmured, 'Goodnight.' Normally he would hold her in his arms until they both went to sleep. She had a long way to go still, she thought hollowly.

Things improved a little over the following few days. With Brad, at any rate. Kerry remained as adamantly against her as ever. Lauren began to doubt that she'd ever break through this new barrier her daughter had erected.

Whatever business affairs Brad had been headed for on Monday, he said nothing about going to town again. He was companionable enough on the surface, though the wicked sparkle no longer danced in his eyes when he looked at her.

'No matter how you feel about your parents, you have to tell them about Kerry,' he said on the Thursday afternoon when they were out riding. 'Even if only by letter.'

'They won't want to know,' Lauren protested. 'So far as they're concerned, they never had a granddaughter to start with.'

'I still think they're entitled. What they choose to do about it is their affair.' He glanced her way, mouth twisting. 'Assuming you haven't been lying about them too.'

'No, I haven't.' She gave a short laugh, not feeling in the least humorous about it. 'Not that I can blame you for suspecting it. I've proved myself a liar through and through!'

'But a lovely one,' he returned drily.

'Does that make me any easier to forgive?' she asked, and saw a corner of his mouth turn down.

'It helps. Kerry has different priorities. You don't seem to be getting any further with her.'

'If anything, I think things are worse,' Lauren admitted wryly. 'She's realised she's going to be stuck with me taking her to and picking her up from Brookfields every day, when you're not here to do it.'

'There's always a chance they haven't filled her place at Thurston yet,' he said.

'I don't think that would be a solution.'

'Then she'll just have to adjust.' He sounded abrupt.
'I'm going ahead. Caliph needs a good fast gallop.
We'll wait for you by the fork.'

He was off almost before he'd finished speaking,
body easy in the saddle as he let the stallion have his
head. Realising he probably wanted to be on his own
for a while, Lauren held Jasper to a canter. Things might
have improved between them, but they were still far
from what they had been. He simply didn't trust her
any more.

Mick was in the tack room when they got back to
the stables. Lauren thought he looked a bit shifty on
emerging. If he had a girlfriend in there again, she
didn't want to know. She had enough problems already
on her plate. They left him to put the horses back in the
paddock with Diamond.

Kerry was in the pool along with Adrian and two
others recognisable from the barbecue. Lauren doubted
if she would have invited them over in view of the
situation, but was glad, for her sake, that they were here.
She needed the companionship.

The day wore on. Dinner was fast becoming a cus-
tomary battle to maintain a semblance of harmony when
Mrs P was around. A probable waste of effort in
Lauren's view. The housekeeper had to be well aware
by now that things were far from right.

The letter Brad had suggested proved even more difficult to write than anticipated. She'd stopped actively
hating her parents a long time ago, but there was no
depth of love there either. In the end, she just set out
the facts of the matter from start to finish, closing with
the hope that they could all get together some time in
the not too distant future.

That there was going to be a future for the three of

them here, she was determined. She hadn't come this
far to give up now.

There was an element of tenderness back in Brad's
lovemaking that night. Lauren's heart warmed to the
gentle kisses he pressed to her eyes and temples before
easing his weight from her. Unlike the last few nights,
he didn't turn away, but turned to her instead, tucking
his knees in behind hers so that they lay together like
a pair of spoons, his arm about her waist, hand covering
her breast.

'Sleep,' he said softly.

She lay awake for some time after he'd drifted off,
allowing herself a cautious optimism. If he could believe in her again, then so could Kerry. However long
it might take.

It was still dark when she opened her eyes again.
Only just three, she saw by the bedside clock.

Brad had shifted onto his back, his breathing deep
and regular. Outlined against the paler square of the
window, his profile looked carved by a master crafts-
man. The sheet had been pushed away, revealing the
broad bare chest with its wiry mat of hair tapering down
to hard-packed stomach. Unseen, the rest of him was
etched on her mind's eye, bringing an urge to reach out
to him, to waken him, to have him part of her again.

She resisted with an effort, not yet quite sure enough
of his feelings to go that far. Too restless to sleep again,
she slid from the bed, careful not to disturb him. The
night was fine. A walk might settle her.

She put on a pair of trousers and a lightweight
sweater along with a pair of pumps. The house was
silent—a little eerie in the shafted moonlight. She went
out via the terrace, dropping down to the lawns with no
particular route in mind.

It was pleasantly warm, with just a hint of a breeze. There was no cloud in the sky, and little industrial haze to dim the stars. The luck of the devil some would call it, Lauren thought, to be given all this, but it wouldn't mean a thing without Brad and Kerry to share it with.

For a moment she took the glow she could see through the trees to be sunrise, realising it was not only far too early but in entirely the wrong direction. Her heart missed a beat as her mind supplied the answer. The stables! It had to be the stables!

The tack room was fully ablaze when she got there, the horses going frantic in their boxes at the smoke and heat already reaching them. Lauren let Diamond out first, then Jasper, sending the two of them galloping into the night.

Caliph was furthest from the blaze, though far from the calmest of the three. Whinnying, snorting, kicking the sides of the box, he was more dangerous than the fire itself, but with the latter already beginning to advance along the row, she couldn't leave him. She tried to calm him a little by talking to him, to absolutely no avail. In the end there was only one thing to do and that was open the lower door. Providing she kept it between them she would be OK, she assured herself.

What she hadn't reckoned with was the size and strength of the animal. When he did come out he almost took the door with him, barging her over. She felt her head come into contact with something hard, and heard a rushing sound in her ears, then everything faded.

She came round to the sound of a voice saying her name. Brad's voice, she realised. It was his arm supporting her, his chest her cheek was pressed against. The roaring sound in the background brought memory flooding back.

'The horses!' she gasped.

'They're fine!' Brad tightened his hold on her. 'Stay still! You may have concussion!'

Her head certainly ached, but her vision was clear enough. Some distance away, the stables were ablaze from end to end, the flames shooting high into the sky. She had to have been out for several minutes for that to happen.

'I'm all right,' she said. 'Really! How did you know?'

'Something woke me. A sound, a premonition...' He broke off, shaking his head, his face bronzed by the flames. 'It doesn't matter how. If I hadn't followed you...' He stopped again, drawing a harsh breath. 'You were lying right up against the wall. Another few minutes, and you'd have been in the thick of it.' He drew her closer still, bending to put his lips to her temple, emotion spilling from him. 'If you'd died...'

'That's the third sentence you've failed to finish,' Lauren joked weakly, unwilling to take the concern of the moment for anything more meaningful. 'I didn't, anyway, thanks to you. Did you call the fire brigade?'

A stupid question, she acknowledged at once, considering the only phone was in the tack room, and the unlikelihood of his carrying a mobile in the tracksuit bottoms he was wearing.

'There isn't much point,' he said. 'It's too late to save anything. Luckily the trees aren't close enough to catch. I'm going to get you back to the house,' he added decisively.

'I can walk!' she protested as he hoisted her up. 'Really, Brad!'

'I'm not taking any chances till you've been seen by a medic,' he said. 'Just relax.'

Relax? Lauren wanted suddenly to laugh. Hysteria, she thought. The arms holding her were so strong, so safe, the face above them so utterly dear to her.

'I love you,' she whispered. 'You have to believe me. I love you!'

'I do,' he said. 'I love you too.' His smile was a caress in itself. 'I was a fool for ever doubting you.'

Eyes like stars, she murmured, 'You did have some reason. I'd have probably doubted me too in your place.'

The smile widened. 'Concussion, maybe, confused, definitely!'

They emerged from the woodland to cross the grass to the terrace. The girl standing there in pyjamas came running down the steps to meet them, her face a study in horror.

'I saw the fire from my window! It's the stables, isn't it? Is Lauren badly hurt?'

'I'm fine,' Lauren assured her, comforted beyond measure that the horses weren't her daughter's first thought.

'You can't be, or Dad wouldn't be carrying you!' The young voice was frantic. 'We have to get a doctor!'

'Put me down, Brad,' Lauren commanded.

He did so without argument, catching her by the arm when she stumbled a little, but not holding her back. Kerry came into her arms like a homing pigeon, the tears sliding down her cheeks.

'I'm sorry I've been so horrible to you! I don't want you to go away! Not ever!'

'I'm not going anywhere.' Lauren was crying herself, overwhelmed by emotion. She had her daughter, she had her husband, she had everything!

*   *   *

Arriving within half an hour of being called, the doctor diagnosed a mild degree of concussion for Lauren, and suggested bed rest. With the sun already up by then, and far better things to do with the day, Lauren said no way. Stubborn as a mule, Brad declared, but he made no attempt to force the issue.

It was necessary to call the brigade out in order to make the smouldering remains safe from flare-up. The safety officer's observation that discarded cigarettes were the most frequent cause of accidental fires sparked a memory for Lauren of the guilty look she'd caught on Mick's face when he'd come from the tack room the previous afternoon.

She didn't mention it to Brad, who would have gone up in flames himself at the mere suggestion, just made a mental note to let the obviously devastated young man know she had her suspicions in order to safeguard the new stables when they were built. In the meantime, a temporary shelter was erected for all three animals in the paddock.

Kerry had changed beyond recognition from the termagant of the last few days. She couldn't do enough.

'I thought you'd only come because you found out how rich Daddy is,' she said when the two of them were on their own.

'And he thought I'd only married him to stay with you,' Lauren smiled. 'The truth being, I wanted to stay with you both so badly by then I lost sight of everything else.' She put out a hand to smooth the blonde hair from her daughter's face, seeing the emerging resemblance to her own with a pleasure she hadn't dared allow herself before. 'I know I can never take Claire's place—I wouldn't even try—but I'll do everything I can to make up for all those missing years. I love you so much, Kerry!'

Tears welled in the hazel eyes again. 'I love you too!'

Lauren put her arms about the girl, the way she had so often longed to do these past weeks, holding her close. It had been a long, hard trek, but they were together at last.

'If someone had told me six months ago that my life was going to turn out like this, I'd have thought they were round the bend!' she exclaimed in bed that night. 'I still keep thinking I'm going to wake up and find it was all a dream!' She gave a yelp as Brad pinched her, looking into the laughing blue eyes in mock-indignation. 'What was that for?'

'Just proving it's no dream,' he said. 'Not that what we just did wasn't out of this world!'

'*Right* out,' she agreed. She drew his head down to kiss him on the lips that gave her so much pleasure. 'You're a lover without equal, Mr Laxton!'

'With you, it isn't hard,' he said, dissolving into laughter again as she raised a suggestive eyebrow. 'There are pitfalls everywhere!'

Amusement gave way to something infinitely more heart-stirring as he studied her captivating face framed by the spread of golden hair across the pillow. 'I'm the luckiest man alive to have you. Especially after the way I treated you this last week.'

Lauren put a finger to his lips. 'We got through it, that's all that matters. You might even say,' she added, 'that we owe Maureen a vote of thanks for bringing it all out in the open.' She gave a wry smile. 'Feminine intuition spurred by animus! She was one of the worst name-callers when it first came out that I was pregnant.'

'Jealousy,' he said. 'With every reason—unless she was a great deal better-looking as a girl than she is now. A nasty piece all round!'

'Over and done with.' Lauren had no intention of wasting any more thought on the woman. 'I've nothing to fear from anyone now. You know everything there is to know about me.'

'Not nearly,' he said softly. 'But I've a lifetime ahead to learn.'

EPILOGUE

'HEAD her over here,' called Brad, brandishing the new camcorder. 'I want a close-up of you both!'

The boy astride the chestnut pony waved a hand in response, and edged the stocky little Shetland in the required direction, gaining a shout of protest from the diminutive rider.

'I can do it myself!'

'It's all right, Paul, let her come on her own,' Lauren called, smothering any trepidation. At four, Chloe was already on her second pony—the first having proved much too docile for her. This one had spirit in abundance, but so did she: evidenced now in the determined way she turned her somewhat self-willed mount in the required direction.

Three years her senior, and wearing the indulgent expression of older brother for younger sister, Paul followed behind on the chestnut, thick dark hair flicked forward over his forehead by the breeze cutting through the paddock.

'Try circling him,' Brad instructed as his young daughter pulled up in front of him. Standing on the lower rung of the fence, he shot a lengthy sequel, panning after her as both pony and rider lost interest in doing something so repetitive and headed back towards mid-field.

'She'll be fine,' he assured Lauren, stepping down from the fence. 'The confidence of youth,' he added with a grin. 'I remember the first time *we* went riding.'

'*I* didn't have the grounding,' she returned in mock-indignation, breaking into laughter to add, 'Not until I met that rabbit, at any rate!'

'Yes, good old Jasper!' His voice was reminiscent. 'He'd have been twenty-four this year.'

'Well, at least Caliph's still with us. Kerry wouldn't have time to ride Diamond these days, even if she was too.'

'No,' he agreed proudly. 'She's really set on becoming a vet.' Eyes on their son and daughter out in the paddock, he added, 'It's still sometimes hard to believe she's in her twenties now. A pity we see so little of her, but that's the way it is when they're grown up and making their own way in the world.'

'I know,' Lauren said softly. 'I miss her too. She'll be home for Easter though—maybe with this new boyfriend she's so close-mouthed about. I just hope he's a decent sort, that's all.' She gave a sigh. 'We've been so lucky, Brad! Ten whole years of wedded bliss!'

He gave her an ironic glance. 'Not what you were thinking this morning when you called me a domineering brute!'

Lauren pulled a face at him. 'Well, you do tend to get on your high horse when it comes to who decides what's what. I'm no docile little housewife ready to accept your word in everything.'

'Tell me about it.' He was grinning. 'Not that I'd want you to be. Can't think of anything more boring than a docile woman! Especially in bed,' he added with that wicked glint in his eyes. 'You were pretty wild last night!'

He viewed the colour springing in her cheeks with amusement. 'And she can still blush, after all these years!'

'You're enough to make a cat blush!' she retorted. 'Anyway, it's time I went and started dinner.'

'You know you don't have to,' he said. 'The woman Mrs P recommended when she retired comes with pretty high qualifications.'

'I'm enjoying playing housekeeper myself for the present. It's hardly as if I've all the cleaning to do as well. Or are you hinting that my cooking doesn't come up to standard, by any chance?'

'As if I'd dare!' His expression softened as he studied the lovely lines of her face framed by the still luxuriant dark gold tresses. 'Joking aside, I can't imagine life without you, Lauren.'

The same way she felt about him, she thought mistily. Apart from a touch of silver in the dark hair, the years had made very little difference. His jawline was just as firm, his body as taut as it had been when she first knew him. He was still a superb lover—as the *frisson* running the length of her spine at the mere thought could testify—and a wonderful father. What more could a woman want?

'I love you,' she said, and saw the blue eyes take on the special glow reserved for her alone.

'Steve can chair tomorrow's meeting,' he said. 'I'm staying right here with my wife and family.'

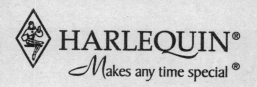

HARLEQUIN®

Makes any time special®

 HARLEQUIN®

AMERICAN *Romance*

Upbeat, All-American Romances

HARLEQUIN®

Duets™

Romantic Comedy

 **Harlequin® Historical**

Historical, Romantic Adventure

HARLEQUIN®

INTRIGUE

Romantic Suspense

Harlequin Romance®

Capturing the World You Dream Of

HARLEQUIN® *Presents*

Seduction and passion guaranteed

HARLEQUIN® *Super*ROMANCE®

Emotional, Exciting, Unexpected

HARLEQUIN® *Temptation*

Sassy, Sexy, Seductive!

HARLEQUIN®
INTRIGUE

WE'LL LEAVE YOU BREATHLESS!

If you've been looking for thrilling tales of contemporary passion and sensuous love stories with taut, edge-of-the-seat suspense—then you'll love Harlequin Intrigue!

Every month, you'll meet four new heroes who are guaranteed to make your spine tingle and your pulse pound. With them you'll enter into the exciting world of Harlequin Intrigue— where your life is on the line and so is your heart!

THAT'S INTRIGUE— ROMANTIC SUSPENSE AT ITS BEST!

HARLEQUIN®
Makes any time special ®

HARLEQUIN®
Makes any time special ®

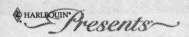